The FARMERS' MARKET MISHAP

A SEQUEL TO *The Lopsided Christmas Cake*

The FARMERS' MARKET MISHAP

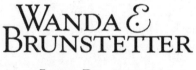

WANDA & BRUNSTETTER

& JEAN BRUNSTETTER

SHILOH RUN PRESS

An Imprint of Barbour Publishing, Inc.

ISBN 978-1-63409-932-5

eBook Editions:
Adobe Digital Edition (.epub) 978-1-68322-353-5
Kindle and MobiPocket Edition (.prc) 978-1-68322-354-2

All scripture quotations are taken from the King James Version of the Bible.

All Pennsylvania Dutch words are taken from The Revised Pennsylvania German Dictionary.

This book is a work of fiction. Names, characters, places, and incidents are either products of the authors' imagination or used fictitiously. Any similarity to actual people, organizations, and/or events is purely coincidental.

Cover image: Richard Brunstetter III: RBIII Studios
Cover Design: Buffy Cooper

Published by Shiloh Run Press, an imprint of Barbour Publishing, Inc., P.O. Box 719, Uhrichsville, OH 44683, www.shilohrunpress.com

Our mission is to publish and distribute inspirational products offering exceptional value and biblical encouragement to the masses.

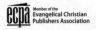 Member of the
Evangelical Christian
Publishers Association

Printed in Canada.

Dedication

To Miriam Brunstetter, and in loving memory of her husband,
Charles Brunstetter—both have always been a beacon
of light to our family. And to our Amish friends,
the Wagler family. Thanks for your warm hospitality.

And let us not be weary in well doing:
for in due season we shall reap, if we faint not.
Galatians 6:9

Chapter 1

Topeka, Indiana

A bone-chilling wind lashed at the trees, scattering bits of debris across the yard. Elma Hochstetler drew her shawl tighter, shivering against the cold. All day long the weather had been like this. One would never know it was the first week of May. She quickened her footsteps, pausing to step around a puddle left from last night's rain. If this unpredictable, windy and gray-skied weather kept up, she'd never get the rest of her garden planted. Hurriedly, she made her way to the chicken coop, not wanting to spend any more time out here than necessary. With nightfall approaching, Elma felt the temperature dropping.

As she passed the barn, Elma heard her trusty horse, Pearl, whinny and kick the door from inside her stall. Cupping her hands around her mouth, Elma hollered, "You're okay, girl; it's just the wind." She grabbed at the scarf covering her head, hoping it wouldn't be blown away, and blinked several times when her eyes began to run because of the stinging air.

When the kicking stopped, Elma breathed a sigh of relief and hurried on. The last thing she needed was one more repair to take care of. The wind followed as she opened the door to the chicken coop, barely making it inside before it slammed shut. Loose feathers stirred up and floated slowly down as the air calmed inside. Sounds of watery clucking, claws scratching the floor, and the fluttery ruffle as a chicken preened itself greeted her. She sneezed when the odor of straw and dusty feed reached her nostrils. Elma blew a feather away from her face that until now, had been stuck in her head scarf.

Collecting eggs wasn't Elma's favorite pastime, nor did she enjoy feeding and watering the unpredictable chickens. She glanced around quickly, hoping Hector wasn't lying in wait for her this evening. The feisty multicolored rooster could be so erratic—sometimes creeping up on her in a sneak attack, other times boldly pursuing her as soon as she stepped into the coop.

Elma looked down at her leg, now sporting an itchy bandage. For no apparent reason, other than just plain orneriness, Hector had pecked her ankle and broken the skin earlier this morning when she'd entered the coop. This evening she'd brought an old broom in with her and made sure it was within reach in case she needed to defend herself. "You won't get me twice today," Elma muttered. "I'm ready for you this time, Hector."

Elma lifted her wicker basket and started down the line. "All right, ladies, what do you have for me?" She'd fed and watered the chickens this morning but hadn't taken time to collect the eggs, as she'd been in a hurry to open the store. The fabric sale going on this week was bringing more customers than they'd expected.

When Elma's twin sister lived here, taking care of the chickens had been her job. But since Thelma married Joseph and they'd moved into the house across the street, she had faced other responsibilities, not to mention the task of caring for her own chickens. And now Thelma was expecting a baby and tired easily. Even though she still helped in the store, for the last month she'd only been working part-time. This put more stress on Elma, as she couldn't manage everything on her own. Two weeks ago, she'd hired Anna Herschberger to help out during the times Thelma couldn't be there. So far, the arrangement had been working well.

"Okay, Gert, you'd better move aside." Elma gave the hen a gentle push, reached into the nesting box, and plucked out a nicely rounded tan-colored egg. "*Danki*, Gert."

Smiling, Elma moved on to the next nesting box, always wary of Hector. No sign of him yet, so she figured he hadn't come inside with the rest of the chickens when the sun began to set.

When Elma finishing gathering eggs, she hurried out the door and headed for the warmth of the house. She'd no more than stepped onto the porch when Tiger showed up. Purring in a deep, throaty rumble, the orange-and-white cat rubbed against her leg. As Elma switched the basket into her other hand, Tiger walked a figure-eight motion in and around her feet.

"Okay, okay, don't be in such a rush. At least allow me to open the door." She turned the knob, and as the door swung open, Tiger released several rapid-fire *meows* and darted in with a swish of his tail, causing Elma to trip. She regained her balance just in time to avoid dropping the eggs. "Tiger, why can't you be more patient? I could have spilled all the eggs and had a big mess to clean up."

Tiger offered a piercing *meow* and paraded off.

Elma rolled her eyes. She'd never cared much for cats, but with the mouse problem she'd had since living in her grandparents' old house, it was either allow the cat in or set traps in most of the rooms. Since Elma began letting Tiger in every evening, the mouse population had decreased, so at least something good had come from it. Elma's twin was the one who loved cats. If Thelma had her way, she'd adopt every stray cat from Topeka to Shipshewana.

Elma entered the kitchen and set the basket of eggs on the counter. She grimaced, noticing the wet tea bag she'd left on a spoon this morning before leaving to open the store. It wasn't like her to be so careless. "Guess I have too much on my mind these days," she murmured, removing her shawl and folding it neatly over the back of a chair.

Tiger, who'd joined her in the kitchen, swished his tail across the hem of Elma's long dress. *Meow. Meow.* It was a definite "I want to be fed now" meow.

"Hang on. I'll get you something to eat shortly." Elma picked up the wilted tea bag and threw it in the garbage. Then she opened a cupboard door to get the cat food. Before she could get the bowl filled, Tiger began gobbling it up.

"You greedy *katz*." Elma chuckled. "You ate breakfast this morning, so you can't be that hungry." She gave him some fresh water then took care of the eggs. Once they were put in the refrigerator, Elma took out a container of leftover vegetable-beef soup, poured it into a kettle, and placed it on her new propane-operated stove. Even unheated, the meaty scent made her stomach growl. Thank goodness the old woodstove was gone, although the kitchen wasn't as warm and toasty now. That sooty old beast had given her and Thelma so much trouble when they'd first moved here after their grandparents died. A good many desserts had flopped or ended up overly brown when they'd baked in the antiquated oven.

Elma snickered, thinking about the lopsided cake her twin sister had made and they'd taken to Shipshewana to be auctioned off. Patting her cheek, it was hard not to get flustered again. Even so, with all the time that had passed, her face grew increasingly warmer with the thought of what had transpired onstage. She could have died of embarrassment when the bidding began. Then, she stood, too stunned to speak, when someone bid one hundred dollars for their pathetic-looking cake. Turned out that Joseph Beechy had convinced his friend Delbert Gingerich to bid on the cake so he could meet Thelma. The plan worked, too, because it didn't take long for Joseph and Thelma to begin courting.

As Elma stirred the soup, her thoughts drifted yet again. Slowly but surely, this old house was being transformed into a more comfortable place to live. At least Elma saw it that way. Grandma and Grandpa had been content to live here a good many years, getting by with what they had and making only a few updates. Even with the new stove, some updated kitchen cabinets, and a new water heater, Elma had a list of things she still wanted to have done. One in particular was getting someone to fix the leaky toilet in the bathroom upstairs. She also hoped to buy a new kitchen table and replace the faded kitchen linoleum, which had worn nearly through in several places—especially in front of the stove. Another project involved carpentry, so she'd need to call on Joseph's friend Delbert for that.

At one time, Delbert and Elma had been a courting couple, but things didn't work out between them. He was too set in his ways, and most likely, he thought she was, too. Then Delbert's cousin Myron Bontrager came on the scene and courted Elma for a few months.

Myron lived in southern Indiana, and it didn't take Elma long to realize a long-distance relationship wasn't going to work out. Besides, she and Myron didn't have much in common, so she wasn't too upset when they went their separate ways.

While waiting for the soup to heat, Elma set the table and poured a glass of water. When the soup was ready, she poured the steaming medley into a bowl, inhaling its beefy aroma. There was only enough for one helping, but it was plenty for her and certainly hearty. After adding a box of crackers and a leftover cheese ball to the setting, she took a seat and bowed her head for silent prayer. *Heavenly Father, I thank You for this food and ask You to bless it to the nourishment of my body. Be with my sister and her husband, and with our family in Sullivan, Illinois. Continue to give me the strength to keep Grandma and Grandpa's store going, and if it be Your will, bring the right man into my life. Amen.*

When Elma opened her eyes, her gaze came to rest on the vacant chair where Thelma used to sit. The chair wasn't the only thing deserted, however. The entire house seemed empty without her presence.

When Elma gave her blessing for Thelma to marry Joseph, she had no idea how lonely it would be to live in this rambling old house all alone. There was no one to converse with except the cat, and cooking for one was certainly no fun. Sometimes during a long, solitary night, Elma would cry herself to sleep. She never let on, though. No point upsetting her sister or throwing cold water on Thelma's happiness.

I need to quit feeling sorry for myself. Elma grabbed the saltshaker and sprinkled a bit on her soup. *My twin deserves to be happy with Joseph. I only wish I could find a man with whom I'd be content—someone who shares my interests and looks at life the way I do.*

Thirty-four and still unmarried, Elma had accepted her plight. Unless God brought the special man to her, she'd be an old maid for the rest of her life.

∽

Thelma sat in the rocking chair, knitting a pair of green booties. The baby wouldn't be here for five more months, but she wanted to be prepared. She glanced at her husband, sitting across from her reading the recent edition of *The Connection* magazine, and smiled.

Returning her smile, Joseph set his magazine aside. "Is the gas lamp giving you enough light?"

"*Jah*, it's plenty."

"I was looking at you a bit ago and noticed you were squinting." He gestured to the coffee table. "You oughta be using those readers right there on the table, don't you think?"

Thelma nodded. "You're right. I'm trying to use what little sight I have without them." She wrinkled her nose. "Anyway, those glasses make me feel like I'm getting old." She began rocking in rhythm to the clicking of her knitting needles.

"You're *schee*. In fact, I think you've gotten even cuter since I married you." Joseph winked at her. "And you're even more beautiful now that you are carrying our baby. You have a glow about you."

She placed the needles in her lap and flapped her hand at him. "Go on now—you're such a tease."

Joseph left his chair and came over to give her a kiss. "I'm not teasing. I'm a lucky man to have found a woman as pretty as you. You're *schmaert*, too."

Thelma bobbed her head. "Now that's one thing I'll have to agree on. I was smart enough to marry you."

He gave her another wink. "Think I'll pour myself a glass of grape juice. Can I get you anything?"

"Juice sounds good. *Danki*, Joe."

"No problem." Joseph gave Thelma another quick kiss and headed for the kitchen.

While Thelma waited for his return, she thought about some of the things she needed to get done before the week was out. Tomorrow was Thursday, and she'd be helping Elma in the store, so not much at home would get done. Friday would have to be laundry day, and Saturday she hoped to do some baking and cleaning.

Thelma felt thankful her utility room was on the main floor. She didn't miss those days of going down to the basement to wash a load of clothes. *Poor Elma. She never has liked going to the basement to do the laundry. It's too bad there isn't a place for her washing machine upstairs.*

Maybe Joe or Delbert could figure something out.

Thelma glanced around the living room. She couldn't help comparing her and Joe's home to Grandpa and Grandma's old house. The fireplace mantel in this home was nicely stained, and the flooring was in tip-top shape. The prior owners had obviously kept the place up.

When Thelma and Joseph first moved in, Elma donated a few pieces of furniture, such as the rocker Thelma sat in now. Of course, Joseph brought the furniture he had in his previous home, so they didn't really need much.

She glanced at the empty cradle sitting across the room. Even though carpentry was not his specialty, Joseph had made the cradle, finishing it last week. Of course, his good friend Delbert, being a carpenter by trade, had given Joe several tips. *What a shame things didn't work out for Dell and Elma.* Thelma got the chair moving faster. *I'd always hoped when I fell in love, my twin sister would find her soul mate and fall in love, too. It would be nice if Elma was also married and expecting a* boppli. *Well, at least she'll have the privilege of being an auntie soon.*

Despite Thelma's love for Joseph, it had been difficult for her to get married and move out of Grandpa and Grandma's old house, leaving Elma alone to fend for herself. Although Thelma and Joseph only lived across the street, it sometimes felt like miles between them. *I wonder what Elma is doing tonight?* Thelma paused from rocking to glance out the front window. During the day, from where she sat now, she could see across the street to the house she'd become so familiar with. Now she could only see a faint light glowing in one of the windows. *It must be lonely for her over there by herself. Well, at least she lives close and we get to see each other nearly every day.*

Thelma and Elma had always been close, and when they'd moved to Topeka two years ago, to take over Grandma and Grandpa's store and live in their house, it had drawn them even closer. She was ever so happy being married to Joseph, but oh, how Thelma wished her twin could find such a wonderful man.

"Oh, my." Thelma's eyes flew open when her neck snapped back before almost nodding off to sleep.

"You look tired, my love." Joseph set a glass of juice on the coffee table near Thelma. "Should we drink our juice and then get ready for bed?"

Thelma yawned, rubbing her neck. "I suppose it would be a good idea. The sale will continue at the store tomorrow so I need to be there early to help Elma."

Joseph's thick eyebrows rose high on his forehead. "I thought Elma hired Anna Herschberger to help out."

"She did, but one of Anna's friends is getting married tomorrow, so Anna asked for the day off." Thelma drank the juice; then, grasping the armrests, she rose from her chair.

Joseph pulled Thelma into his arms and kissed her tenderly. "I love you so much, and now that you're expecting a boppli, I want to be sure you take good care of yourself."

She tipped her head back, reaching up to stroke his soft beard. "Now don't look so worried. I'll be fine, Joe, and so will our baby."

Chapter 2

"You look *mied* this morning. Are you sure you feel up to working today?" Elma placed both hands on her sister's shoulders.

"I am a bit tired, but with the sale going on still, and Anna not working, you need my help." Thelma smiled, although it didn't quite reach her usual sparkling blue eyes. "Besides, I enjoy being here in the store with you and having the opportunity to visit with customers."

Elma knew all about her twin's eagerness to visit. Even when they were children, Thelma had been the outgoing one. While Elma was talkative with people she knew, her sister easily carried on conversations with complete strangers. She remembered how once, when they were ten years old, their mother had taken them shopping. As they were getting ready to leave the store, Thelma walked right up to a young English girl and asked where she'd gotten her red balloon. The next thing Elma knew, her sister and the English girl were exchanging addresses so they could write to each other. Elma had never understood why she and Thelma were different on many levels. Yet they were as close as any identical twins could possibly be.

"I have a suggestion." Elma moved to one side of the stool where her sister sat. "Why don't you sit on this stool here by the counter and wait on people? I'll take care of cutting material and restocking shelves as needed."

"Are you sure? I can help stock shelves if you need me to."

Elma shook her head determinedly. "Absolutely not! In your delicate condition, you should not be doing anything strenuous. At least here by the counter, you can stay off your feet."

"You and Joseph worry about me too much." Thelma folded her arms across her stomach. "I'm not an invalid, you know."

"Of course not, but you're thirty-four years old and expecting your first boppli. You need to be careful and not overwork." Elma glanced down at her sister's ankles then quickly looked away. She wasn't about to mention the slight swelling she'd noticed. Thelma would think she was fussing too much. But if it got any worse, she wouldn't hesitate to speak up.

Thelma sighed. "All right, I'll do as you say."

"Good to hear." Elma put the OPEN sign in the large front window and had barely gotten the door unlocked when a horse and buggy pulled up. Four Amish ladies got out, and, as soon as the horse was secured, they hurried into the store. One of them, whom Elma had not met before, held a baby in her arms. For a split second Elma felt a pang of jealousy, but she quickly got it under control.

"*Guder mariye.*" Elma greeted them with a smile.

"Good morning. How are you today, Thelma?" Clara Lehman gave Elma a hug.

Elma shook her head. "Oh, no, I'm not Thelma. I'm Elma."

Clara's cheeks reddened. "Sorry about that. You two look so much alike. Even after two years of knowing you both, it's hard to tell you apart." She looked over at Doris Miller, who stood beside her. "Don't you agree?"

"Jah, but then Thelma is the one expecting a boppli, so we should be able to tell them apart." Doris motioned to Elma's stomach and snickered. "Does she look like she's in a family way?"

"Of course not." Clara's face colored further, and Elma's cheeks heated as well. She pushed up the left sleeve of her dress, revealing a small scar on her elbow. "One way you can always tell us apart is by this scar. I got it when I was a child and fell off my bike."

"And don't forget the small mole I have behind my right ear," Thelma called from her place behind the counter. "It's one sure way to know who is who."

Clara chuckled as she moved toward the counter. "Now, now,

Thelma, most people would not be likely to look behind your ear."

"Or see the scar on Elma's arm," Doris interjected.

This discussion was getting nowhere, and Elma was about to ask if either of the ladies needed help with anything, when the door opened again and two more women entered the store. From the looks of things, today would be busy. That was good; Elma liked being busy. She moved across the room to introduce herself to the young woman with the baby, while Doris, Clara, and the other women stood at the counter talking with Thelma.

⌒

By noon, Thelma felt more than ready to take a break. She'd been waiting on customers all morning, and her back was beginning to hurt from sitting so long. She noticed her ankles appeared to be a bit swollen today. It was hard to believe, but twenty customers had come into the store in the last hour, all looking for material and sewing notions. Thelma wondered if every woman in their community had gone shopping today.

She stepped off the stool, and was about to seek Elma out to say she wanted to go to the back room to eat lunch, when Lizzie Yoder entered the store. Ambling over to the counter, the older woman asked breathlessly, "Does the sale you're having include everything in the store?" Her blue eyes seemed to grow larger. "I hope so, because I need a few things and don't have much money to spend."

"I'm sorry," Thelma responded, "but only the bolts of material are on sale today."

Lizzie's double chin tilted downward as she heaved a sigh. "I figured as much but had to ask. Guess I'll head on down the notions aisle."

Thelma watched Lizzie walk away. For a sixty-two-year-old who was a bit on the pudgy side, Lizzie moved pretty fast. *I hope I'm that full of energy when I'm her age.*

Once again, Thelma was on the verge of calling her sister to mind the counter when Mary Lambright entered the store. "It's good to see you. How are your boys doing these days?" Thelma asked.

Mary's eyes brightened. "Philip and Richard are doing well. They both enjoy being in school."

"I'll bet they do. Seems like just yesterday when they were sitting here in the store listening to me read them a story."

Mary bobbed her head. "My *kinner* have grown so quickly." She motioned to Thelma. "Bet you're looking forward to becoming a *mudder*."

"Oh, jah. Joseph and I are both excited about becoming parents." Thelma looked down at her growing stomach and patted it gently.

Mary smiled. "Guess I'd better get what I came in here for. If you're still at the counter when I'm ready to pay for my purchases, we can chat a bit longer."

When Mary hurried off, Thelma stepped down from the stool. She was getting ready to head to the back of the store when Lizzie showed up again. "I'm ready to check out now."

Thelma glanced around, hoping Elma was nearby and would come to her rescue, but no such luck. She must be at the back of the store.

"Umm. . .sure, I can check you out, Lizzie." Thelma stepped behind the counter again, and Lizzie placed her purchases down—a notebook, two spools of black thread, four skeins of green yarn, and a bag of jelly beans. Seeing the candy caused Thelma to think of Joseph's friend Delbert. He seemed to always have candy in his pocket. Delbert had a sweet tooth, for sure. But then from what Thelma had seen, so did Lizzie. *Good thing Elma's not waiting on her. She'd probably give Lizzie a lecture on the danger of eating too much sugar.*

"What's new with you, Lizzie?" Thelma questioned as she put the woman's purchase in a plastic bag.

Lizzie squinted over the top of her glasses. "Nothing good, that's for sure."

"What do you mean?"

"My brother, Abe, will be moving to Kentucky soon, and he's taking his whole family with him." Lizzie touched her chest. "Everyone but me."

"I didn't realize they were leaving the area. Why don't you go with them?"

"I was invited to move, but I said no, I'm staying put." Lizzie shook her head so hard her head-covering ties swished across her face. "Topeka's my home, and there's nothing in Kentucky for me."

Thelma pursed her lips. "So you'll stay here all alone?" Lizzie had never married, and it didn't seem right that she wouldn't live near her family anymore.

Lizzie shrugged her shoulders. "My friend Peggy will be moving in with me soon, and we'll share expenses. We clean houses together, so things should work out okay for both of us." She grabbed the package of jelly beans, ripped it open, and took out a few of the black ones. "These licorice jelly beans are my favorite." She offered Thelma a sheepish grin and popped a handful into her mouth.

Thelma resisted the urge to say something about eating so much candy. She'd be acting like her sister. "Will there be anything else?"

"Nope, that's all for now. I'll see you again soon, though, I expect." Lizzie leaned against the counter and lowered her voice. "So how are you feeling these days? Still having morning sickness?"

"Not anymore, but I do get awful tired at times." Thelma almost snickered. *Funny how some people feel compelled to drop their voice when talking about certain topics.*

"I can't speak from experience, mind you, but I've seen plenty of women who were in a family way. Some have the morning sickness and some don't. Everyone is different." Lizzie ate several more jelly beans of various flavors. "Well, I'd better get going." She paid for her items, picked up the sack, and headed for the door. "Have a nice day, Thelma."

As Lizzie was putting the bag of candy into her satchel, a few jelly beans fell out of the opening. "Don't worry, I'll get them." Lizzie scurried to pick them up. "It's okay. I think I got them all. You take care now."

"You, too." Thelma chuckled. Lizzie Yoder was quite the character. Too bad Lizzie's family would be moving to Kentucky. Thelma couldn't imagine what it would be like if Elma moved away. Of course, that wasn't likely to happen since Elma wasn't married. Even if she was, no way would Thelma's twin sister leave her—especially when she would become an aunt in five months.

⌣

When they had a small break between customers, Elma joined Thelma at the counter. "You've been up here a long while, Sister. You'd best take a break while I keep an eye on things."

"Danki. I'm more than ready for it." Thelma rose from the stool and headed for the back of the store.

Elma followed her into the back room and grabbed her lunch basket to take up front. "I'll eat this while I'm at the counter, in case any customers come in." She gave her sister's arm a gentle pat. "You relax, put your feet up, and take it easy. If I need you, I'll give a holler."

Thelma's appreciation was evident as she took a seat and smiled at Elma. "I was beginning to wonder if things would ever slow down."

Elma chuckled. "You know how it goes. We're either bored and looking for something to do, or the store is literally crawling with customers."

"Jah." Thelma pointed to the door. "You'd better get busy and eat before more people show up."

"Okay, see you soon." Elma hurried to the counter and placed her bologna and cheddar cheese sandwich, along with some carrot and celery sticks, on a napkin. As soon as she removed the thermos lid, the tangy smell of apple juice wafted up to her nose, making her mouth water.

Elma managed to eat most of her lunch before Hazel Zimmerman, one of the Mennonite women who lived close by, stopped by.

"Good day, Elma." Hazel offered a genuine smile. At least she hadn't gotten Elma mixed up with Thelma.

"How are things with you today?" Elma put her lunch basket behind the counter.

"My back has been acting up, but other than that, everything is going pretty well." Hazel reached around and rubbed her lower back.

"Sorry to hear it. I hope your back gets better soon." Elma picked up the spray cleaner and a napkin to tidy the area, while Hazel headed to the fabric section.

A short time later, Hazel returned with a bolt of pale blue, lightly printed material. "Do you happen to have more of this color in the back?"

"I'll go take a look; just give me a second." Elma stepped out from behind the counter and headed for the back room. When she entered, she spotted Thelma dozing in her chair.

Elma smiled. *I'll let her rest awhile longer. My twin needs to take care of herself and not overdo.* She found the material she'd come for and stepped quietly out of the room.

Once outside the door, Elma scurried to find the scissors to cut through the packaging tape. "This isn't going as smoothly as I had hoped," she mumbled quietly. After she had the box opened and began pulling the material out, she could see it wasn't the right material. Elma looked over at the next box sitting nearby and grabbed the scissors again. This time she had the right color, but now she'd created a mess in the back of the store.

Sighing, she heard the door out front open and close, then more voices. She hurried up front where she found Hazel leaning against the fabric table. "I believe this is what you wanted."

Hazel grinned. "Thanks, it's perfect."

Elma pushed her glasses back in place and looked toward the door, where two English women stood. "Hello, ladies."

"Hello," they said in unison.

"We saw your ad in the paper," the older of the two women said, "and we're here to check out your sale."

"Please feel free to look around." Elma gestured to the fabric section of the store.

As the women looked through the material, Elma cut Hazel's fabric and rang up the notions and thread she'd picked out.

"Are you working alone today?" Hazel picked up her bagged purchases.

"No, my sister is here, but she's taking a break." Elma glanced toward the back room, wondering if Thelma was still asleep.

"Well, tell her I said hello, and you have a good day."

"Thanks. You, too."

While the two English women shopped for fabric, Elma knelt to organize the work space behind the counter. Then she heard someone step up behind her.

"Sister, how long were you going to let me sleep?" Thelma tilted her head. "Why are you looking at me so strangely?"

"Your head covering's on crooked." Elma reached out and put it back in place. "And the reason I didn't wake you is because I figured you could use some rest."

"Well, I got some. Have I missed much?" Yawning, Thelma smoothed the front of her dress.

"Hazel Zimmerman came in for material and notions, and a couple of English ladies are looking at material." Elma glanced in their direction.

"I'll pop back there and see if they have any questions."

Elma shook her head. "You should stay off your feet. I'll go see how they are doing." Elma motioned to the wooden stool.

Thelma opened her mouth as if about to argue the point, but with a slight shrug, she took a seat.

As the day wore on, so did Elma's exhaustion. She could see clearly from the distant look in her sister's eyes, and the way she sagged on the stool, that she was still quite weary.

"It's time to close up," Elma said. "Why don't you go on home now? I'll take care of everything."

Thelma didn't argue. She gathered up her things, gave Elma a hug, and with hands hanging limply, headed out the door. "See you tomorrow, Sister."

"You're not working tomorrow," Elma called to Thelma's retreating form. "Anna will be here to help me."

Thelma lifted a hand in a backward wave and shut the door behind her.

Elma slouched against the counter, supporting her head with a hand. Her muscles felt heavy, and her senses dulled. For the last hour she'd had difficulty focusing, and now all she wanted to do was go home, take a hot bath, and sit with her feet propped up. But of course, it was wishful thinking. Even though she'd collected eggs this morning and had given the chickens food and water, other animals needed tending to this evening. Somehow she would push herself to feed the barn cats and check on the horses. After those chores were done, she would grab something from the refrigerator for a quick supper, and if she had enough energy left, she'd take a bath and then put her feet up.

Pulling from deep within, Elma proceeded to turn off the gas lamps and lock up the store for the night. She missed the days when she and Thelma closed the store together then went home and shared a meal, enjoying each other's companionship and the quietness of their house. So much had changed in the last two years. Sometimes it still didn't seem possible that she now lived alone.

Heading down to the house, Elma heard Pearl whinny in the barn. "I'll be back soon to feed you, girl," Elma called.

Like clockwork, Tiger was waiting on the porch to be let in for dinner. "I know you're hungry, Tiger. So am I." Elma reached into her sweater pocket for her key chain but came up empty. She held her hands behind her back, gripping her wrists. *Oh, no. Where did I put the keys? I must have dropped it on the way down to the house.*

She looked down at the cat, who was meowing and rubbing her legs. "Sorry, Tiger, but we aren't going in yet. I have to find my keys."

CHAPTER 3

Tiger's plaintive *Meow!* was almost Elma's undoing. She was hungry, too, and wanted to get in the house as much as he did.

"My keys have to be somewhere between the store and home." Elma's teeth clamped together when she turned and the cat darted between her legs. "Tiger, you're gonna trip me again." She clapped her hands. "Now scat!"

Elma stepped off the porch and headed back to the store, searching the ground as she went. "*Ach*, my back is throbbing." She gripped the area above her hip as she stooped over, scanning more of the area. It was like looking for a sewing needle in a field of hay. Grass, weeds, gravel, and dirt covered the path leading back to the store, and although it may have helped, she wasn't about to crawl on her hands and knees to get a closer look. Besides, the sunlight was slowly fading, making it more difficult to see anything that might be lying on the ground. Maybe the keys were inside the store. If that was the case, she was out of luck. Her key to the store was on the same chain as the one for the house, and she'd flipped the lock on the store before shutting the door. Aside from breaking a window to get inside, it could be all for nothing if the keys weren't there. Elma didn't need to add purchasing a new window to her growing project list.

"So, great!" Elma looked up at the sky in exasperation. "Now both keys are missing."

While she continued her search, Tiger meowed and pawed at the hem of her skirt.

"I'm sorry, Tiger." She bent to pet him. "But I can't feed either of us till I locate those keys. Wish you could help me find them." Elma's eyes teared up. This was a time when she missed having her twin sister at her side. Thelma would probably remain upbeat, saying something like, "Don't worry, Sister, we'll find them."

Elma choked back a sob as she searched the ground, taking small steps toward the store.

After looking for what seemed like hours, she gave up. The only sensible thing was to go over to Thelma's house and borrow her set of keys. "Don't know why I didn't think to do it sooner." She tapped the side of her head, almost knocking her head covering off.

Elma hurried down the driveway, thankful it wasn't windy this evening. She paused at the mailbox to retrieve the mail then, looking both ways, crossed the street. Joseph and Thelma's front room window faced the road, along with most of the wraparound porch. So if her sister wanted to sit outside, she could watch the customers come and go.

As Elma started up the driveway, to go around back, she heard a familiar *meow!* Looking down, she groaned. Much to her chagrin, Tiger had followed her across the street.

$\backsim$

Thelma was about to start supper when Joseph entered the kitchen. "Don't bother fixing anything for us, 'cause I'm takin' my beautiful *fraa* out for supper this evening."

"Oh, Joseph, are you sure? I bet you had a busy day at the harness shop. Wouldn't you prefer to stay home and rest?"

"Nope." He stepped up to Thelma and gave her a hug. "I did have a busy day, but I'm guessin' you did as well. Your stooped posture and red-brimmed eyes are a good indicator of exhaustion."

Thelma nodded. "I used to be able to work five days a week and do all sorts of chores without feeling so *mied*."

Joseph tipped her head back so she was looking directly into his eyes. She giggled when he affectionately tweaked her nose. "But you weren't expecting a *boppli* back then. Which is why you need to take it easy and let me treat you to a meal out at Tiffany's."

Thelma's mouth watered thinking about the good food on the

menu there, not to mention what was available on the restaurant's buffet. "All right, let me wash up and get changed into a clean dress, and I'll be ready to go."

"I need to clean up and change my clothes, too."

They started down the hall toward their bedroom but halted their footsteps when someone pounded on the back door. Thelma went to the door and was surprised to find her sister standing on the porch.

"Can I borrow your key so I can get into my house?" Elma spoke breathlessly, and her cheeks were bright pink.

Thelma blinked rapidly. "What happened to your key?"

"I don't know. I lost it somehow, and since the store key is on the same ring, I don't have it, either. I had them when I locked up the store, so they must have slipped out of my hand somewhere between the store and home." Elma heaved a heavy sigh. "I'm tired, hungry, and so is my pestering cat, so I need to get into the house right away."

"I'll get my key for you." Thelma went to her purse and took out the key. She handed it to her sister then turned to Joseph and whispered, "Would you mind if I invited Elma to go out to supper with us?"

"Course not. She's more than welcome to join us at Tiffany's."

Elma smiled. "It's a nice offer, but I have to feed the animals yet, and. . ."

Joseph held up his hand. "Not a problem. I'll take care of your outside chores while you and my fraa get ready to go out. Once I'm done, I'll come back here, take a quick shower, and change into clean clothes. Then we can be off to Tiffany's."

Elma pushed an unruly strand of hair back under her head covering then picked Tiger up before he decided to venture back across the road. "If you're sure you don't mind, I'd appreciate the help, and a meal out this evening sounds *wunderbaar*."

⁓

Soon after Elma was seated at a table with her sister and brother-in-law, she spotted Delbert Gingerich coming in the door. Joseph must have seen him, too, for he waved Delbert over.

After everyone greeted Delbert, Joseph pointed to the empty chair at their table. "If you're not meeting someone, we'd be glad to have you join us, Dell."

"I'm not meeting anyone, but hey, I don't mind sitting by myself. Sure don't want to interrupt your meal." Delbert rubbed the back of his neck. Shuffling his feet, he glanced at Elma then looked quickly away.

"No one should have to eat alone, especially when their friends are sitting right here." Joseph got up and pulled out the empty chair. "Now I won't take no for an answer."

"Well, umm. . ."

Delbert looked at Elma, as though needing her approval, but before she could form a response, Thelma spoke up. "We'd be pleased if you joined us, Dell. We haven't seen you in a while, and it'll be nice to catch up."

Feeling as if she had no other choice, Elma smiled and nodded. While she had nothing personal against Joseph's friend, his little quirks sometimes got on her nerves. She remembered from when Delbert courted her how stubborn and opinionated he could be. He also ate too much candy and was a poor sport whenever they played a board game with Thelma and Joseph.

Delbert's eyes brightened as he took a seat and slid his chair in close to the table. "Anyone know what the special here is tonight?"

"I'm not sure." Joseph motioned to the buffet. "But that's what I'm goin' for. It's nice to get a variety of food."

Elma glanced in that direction. Joseph was right. There were so many dishes to choose from—chicken, corn, mashed potatoes, thick noodles, a salad bar full of fresh vegetables, and some wonderfully tasty desserts.

"Guess I'll have the buffet, too." Delbert grinned. "I had a busy day and worked up a hearty appetite."

"What are you going to have?" Elma asked her twin.

Thelma shrugged her shoulders. "I am kind of *hungerich*, so I may as well have the same. How about you?"

"Since everyone else is going to the buffet, I will, too."

"Let's have our silent prayer before we help ourselves," Joseph suggested.

Everyone closed their eyes.

Heavenly Father, Elma prayed, *bless this food to the nourishment of our bodies, and please bless everyone at this table. Amen.*

"How are things with you these days, Elma?" Delbert asked as he followed her up to the buffet. "Are you still keeping plenty busy at the store?"

"Jah, I am, and with things at the house, too." She pursed her lips. "There are many items on my list that need to be done, beginning with the upstairs toilet."

"What's wrong with it?"

"It's leaking, and I'm continually wiping up the floor."

His brows pulled together. "Not good, Elma. If you don't get it fixed soon it could damage the bathroom floor, not to mention creating a mold problem."

"I wouldn't want that to happen." She wrinkled her nose. "I've been meaning to ask Joseph, but he's been extra busy in his shop lately, so it may have to wait until things slow down for him."

"Not to worry." Delbert smiled. "I'll drop by your place and take a look at the situation. It might be something I can easily fix." He blushed; then he quickly added, "If it's okay with you, that is."

"Danki. It's kind of you to offer, and I appreciate it. I'll pay you, of course." Elma picked up a clean plate.

"We'll see how it goes. If it doesn't take too much time, I may only charge you for the part." When Delbert picked up a plate, it nearly slipped out of his hands. "Oops." He managed to grab it in time. As he started down the line, he put a glob of mashed potatoes on it then added some gravy. "Everything else okay?"

"Pretty much—except for losing the keys to my house and the store today."

"Did you find them?" He looked at her intently.

Elma shook her head. "I borrowed Thelma's key so I could get into the house, and I'll use her key to the store when I open it tomorrow." She forked a chicken thigh and put it on her plate.

"That's too bad. I hope you find it." Delbert took some of the golden-crusted meat and plopped it next to his potatoes.

"So do I." Elma added some noodles to her plate. "If I don't find them, I'll take Thelma's keys to the hardware store and have some copies made."

Delbert nudged Elma's arm with his elbow. "You can do that all right, but if someone finds the keys you lost, it could be *arig*."

She tipped her head. "Why would it be bad?"

"If the wrong person found your keys, they might break into the house or store and steal from you. If you like, I could change the locks on both doorknobs and get you another set of keys."

Elma gulped. Having Delbert around, for yet another project, could be a little unnerving. Now she was even more determined to find those lost keys.

CHAPTER 4

The following morning, Elma woke up with a pounding head-
ache, as well as a stiff neck. She'd lain awake much of the
night, worrying someone might have found her keys and
would enter her house or rob the store. Every little noise and creak of
the house put Elma on alert.

The first thing she did when she entered the kitchen was to grab
a glass of water and take an aspirin. Then she stepped outdoors and
took care of feeding and watering the animals in the barn. When that
chore was done, she headed to the chicken coop, carrying a basket in
the crook of her arm.

Hearing the shrill cry of a hawk, Elma stopped to watch it cir-
cling on the air currents. A wave of peaceful calm came over her as
she paused to pray. *Lord, help me to do Your will today. Please remind me
to reflect You in all I say and do.*

Things went well in the chicken coop, and Elma returned to the
kitchen with six nice-sized eggs. Her head still hurt, and it almost felt
as though she was in a daze. As she began to prepare breakfast, Elma
wavered as pure exhaustion took over.

Holding on to the countertop, she stood quietly, until her vision
cleared. Then glancing down, she noticed her furry companion, eagerly
lapping the fresh water in his dish. "Sure wish I'd found those keys, Tiger."

The cat looked up at her briefly then began nibbling the food
she'd given him. At least somebody was happy this morning.

Elma went to the refrigerator and took out a carton of eggs.
Think I might feel better if I had a dog to alert me to any danger.

Tiger's only good for catching mice.

As though he could read her thoughts, the cat left his dish and came over to rub against Elma's leg. She couldn't help but smile. "Okay, Tiger, you're a nice pet." Truth was, ever since Thelma moved out, Elma found herself talking to the cat as though he were a friend. At least it was better than talking to herself.

Elma got out the frying pan and cooking oil. She was about to pour some into the pan when she heard a horse's whinny. Glancing out the window, she was surprised to see Delbert's buggy pulling in. Elma watched as he secured his horse to the hitching rail and started for the house.

"Guder mariye," Elma said after opening the door. "What brings you by here this morning?"

Delbert lifted his toolbox and grinned. "Came to take a look at your leaky toilet, and maybe put a new lock on the house and at the store." He stepped into the house and followed her to the kitchen. "That is, unless you've already found your keys."

"No, I haven't, but then I haven't looked for them yet this morning." Elma gestured to the stove. "I was about to fix myself some scrambled *oier*. If you care to join me for breakfast, I'll fix enough for the both of us."

Delbert removed his straw hat and scratched his blond head. "I did have a cup of *kaffi* and a *faasnachtkuche* before I left home, but I could probably eat a plate of scrambled eggs."

Elma resisted the urge to tell Delbert that a doughnut and coffee did not make a healthy breakfast. Instead she smiled and said, "Okay, if you want to go down the hall to the bathroom and wash your hands, I'll get the eggs started."

"Okie-dokie." Delbert set his toolbox on the floor, and as he sauntered off, he sneezed.

Remembering his allergy to cats, Elma picked Tiger up and opened the door. "Sorry I have to do this, but out you go." She placed the cat on the porch and quickly shut the door.

Returning to the kitchen, Elma washed her hands at the sink and got started on the eggs. By the time they were done, Delbert was back.

"Is there a katz in the house?" He glanced around. "I started sneezing as I was going down the hall."

"Tiger was in here, but I put him out, so I hope it helps." Elma set two plates on the table, along with the platter of scrambled eggs and two glasses of orange juice.

"My allergies get so bad, sometimes all it takes is being in a house where a cat's been. It's their dander that affects me."

"I'm sorry about that. If I'd known for sure when you were coming, I would have put Tiger out before you got here."

"It's okay. I'll live." Delbert smacked his lips and pulled out a chair. "Looks good, Elma. Danki for asking me to join you."

"You're welcome." She smiled and took the seat across from him. Following Delbert's lead, Elma bowed her head for silent prayer.

When their prayers ended, they ate and talked about the weather, since Elma couldn't think of anything else to talk about. Being alone with Delbert felt strange. It made her think back to their courting days. Only then, Joseph and Thelma had been with them during all of their outings. Delbert and Elma had only been alone on a few occasions, whenever he'd come over to work on the house.

She reflected on the day he'd found carpenter ants in their porch, and how she'd appreciated his help, then and now. There were times Elma wished things could have worked out between them. *But it must not have been meant to be,* she thought. *Delbert may be a confirmed bachelor for the rest of his life, and I, quite likely, will remain an old maid.*

⌒

As Delbert began working on the toilet, his nose twitched. A musty odor in the room led him to check around. Leaning closer in at the flooring near the back wall next to the toilet base, he took the screwdriver out of his pouch to see what might be going on. Delbert knelt down and poked around the flooring near the wall. It chipped up easily as he pushed the tool into the rotted spot. *This needs to be fixed, and now I know why it smells so nasty in here.* He would bring the situation to Elma's attention when he went out to the store later on.

Delbert thought about Elma, and how tired she looked this morning. Seeing the dark circles beneath her eyes, he had a hunch she'd been working too hard and wasn't getting enough sleep. No doubt her responsibilities had increased after Thelma married Joe and moved out of their grandparents' house. In a place this old, things were bound to fall apart, which meant a lot more maintenance.

He put the screwdriver away then picked up the part he needed for the toilet and set it in place. *I wonder if Elma will ever get married. If she was a little more easygoing, like her sister, she'd have a better chance at snagging a man.* His forehead wrinkled. *She is a fine-looking woman, though. Her silky brown hair and pretty blue eyes are what attracted me to her in the beginning. If she hadn't been so persnickety, our relationship might have gone further.*

Delbert couldn't help but envy his good friend. Seeing the look of adoration that Joe and Thelma exchanged last night was enough to make any man jealous. *I don't want somebody tellin' me what to do, but it sure would be nice to have a pretty wife waiting for me at the end of the day with a sweet smile and a home-cooked meal.*

He thought about the two women he'd gone out with a couple of times since he and Elma broke up. Sarah worked at a gift shop in Shipshewana, and he'd met Millie at the hardware store in LaGrange. They were both nice enough, but the connection wasn't there, so they'd gone their separate ways rather quickly.

"Maybe I'm gettin' too old and set in my ways," Delbert muttered as he finished up with the toilet. "Might be best if I learn to be content with my life as it is now and quit hoping for something that's probably never gonna happen."

He stood and arched his back. *Guess I'd better go out to the store and let Elma know I'm done.*

⌒

Elma had just finished waiting on a customer when Delbert entered the store. "Got the toilet fixed," he announced, stepping up to the counter. "But the bad news is, you'll need some floor work done in the near future. The leak you had was dripping down and rotting out the floor behind the toilet. The bad wood will need to be taken out and replaced with new flooring. There's a disgusting odor coming from there, too. I'm surprised you didn't mention it to me."

She rubbed her forehead and grimaced. "I have noticed the smell but wasn't sure of the cause."

"Well, when you're ready to do the job let me know." Delbert swiped at his brow.

Elma rested her hand on her hip. "I've wanted to replace that old flooring anyway. It's worn and faded looking."

"I'll run back to the house now and get the square footage you'll need for the new linoleum. That way you'll know how much to order." Delbert pulled his fingers through the end of his hair. "I haven't locked up yet, but I'll do that as soon as I'm finished measuring."

"Oh, good. How much do I owe you?" Elma shifted her weight, trying not to stare at his deep blue eyes.

"Nothing for my labor. I left a bill on your kitchen table for the cost of the parts. No hurry about paying me, though. After I get those floor measurements, I'll leave a note on the table with the bill."

"Danki, Delbert. I'm grateful for all you've done."

Placing both hands on the counter, he leaned close and lowered his voice. "Where do you think you lost your keys?"

Elma shook her head. "I looked all along the path between here and the house but came up empty handed." Her gaze flitted around the room. "I hope if someone else found them they'd be kind enough to say something."

"Well, you can't take any chances. I'll head over to the hardware store and get new locks for all the doors on your house, as well as the front and back door here at the store."

"Danki, Delbert." Elma placed her hand on top of his but quickly pulled it away when another customer approached the counter. "When the job's been done, let me know how much I owe you."

"Will do. See you later, Elma."

Elma smiled and lifted her hand in a brief wave. Delbert seemed a lot nicer than when they'd been courting. Maybe he'd learned a few things about how to treat a woman.

ᴄ⸝

As the day wore on, exhaustion set in. Yesterday had been busy, but today it seemed like even more customers had come in. Everyone was looking for a bargain, and their supply of material had diminished to less than half.

Elma sighed. *Hopefully there's another box of material in the back of the store. I should have been more prepared for our sale, but I'll make note of this for the future.* She picked up a pen and slid the notepad in front of her. She jotted down a list of supplies and noted an estimate of how much material had been sold. Her eyelids felt heavy as she released a noisy yawn. On Monday, when the store was usually closed, Elma would place an order for more fabric, as well as several other items she'd run low on.

Elma waved her hand at a pesky bee flying around her head. She noticed a few on the windows as well, buzzing and trying to get out. "With all the customers coming and going, is it any wonder there are *ieme* inside?" She opened the front door and shooed some of them out.

"Are you as mied as I am?" Elma asked when her helper joined her at the counter.

"Jah. It's been a busy, tiring day, that's for sure." Anna tugged at her apron band and cleared her throat. "Umm. . .there's something I have to tell you, Elma."

"You look so serious, Anna. What is it?"

The young woman dropped her gaze to the floor and stood silently several seconds. When she lifted her head again, Elma saw tears in Anna's blue eyes. "I find no pleasure in telling you this, but unfortunately, I can only work for you another two weeks."

Elma's posture stiffened. "How come?"

"My *daed* sold his business and my folks are relocating to Arthur, Illinois, where my grandparents live." Anna's arms hung loose at her sides, and her chin trembled slightly. "I don't really want to move, but my place is with my parents and siblings. Besides, my *grossmudder* is not well, and my *mamm's* going to need my help to take care of Grandma."

Elma reached across the counter and clasped Anna's hand. "You'll be missed, of course, but I understand." Elma had a sinking feeling in the pit of her stomach. There was no way she could expect Thelma to work more than a few days a week, so she'd have to hire someone else.

Trouble was, she had no idea who it could be.

Chapter 5

Grabill, Indiana

Dorothy Wagler glanced at the clock above the refrigerator and frowned. If Ben didn't come in from doing his chores soon she might have to eat breakfast without him, because her driver would be here in thirty minutes.

She peered out the kitchen window but saw no sign of her son. Dorothy tapped her fingers on the edge of the sink then opened a drawer and took out two pot holders. *Sure wish he would hurry. I'm getting hungry, and smelling the buttery, browning casserole is making my mouth water.*

Dorothy went to the refrigerator, took out a pitcher of apple juice, and poured some into two glasses. She picked up her glass and brought it to her lips, savoring the cool, tangy-sweet liquid. "Ahh. . . this hits the spot."

Next, she removed the steaming breakfast casserole from the oven and placed it on the table, glancing at the clock one more time. *Five more minutes, Ben, and then I'm eating without you.*

After placing the silverware and napkins at each plate, Dorothy slid out her chair. She was about to take a seat at the table when her son rushed into the room. Tilting his head to one side, he pushed a piece of thick brown hair out of his eyes. "What were ya gonna do, Mom, eat *friehschtick* without me?"

Dorothy pointed to the clock. "Reba will be here soon, and if I don't eat breakfast now I won't be ready when she arrives."

"What's she's coming for? Do you have another chiropractic appointment?" He rubbed his clean-shaven chin.

"I hired Reba to drive me to Topeka to see my friend Eileen Lehman." Dorothy's mouth slackened. "Don't you remember me telling you this during supper last night?"

Ben shrugged his broad shoulders. "Guess I must've forgot."

Dorothy lifted her gaze toward the ceiling. "Goodness gracious, son, you're only thirty-five years old. Your memory shouldn't be giving out on you already."

He grunted, moving to the sink to wash his hands. "My memory's not giving out, Mom. I just have a lot on my mind."

"I know you do, Ben, and I didn't mean to sound condemning. Sorry if I came off that way." Dorothy gestured to the table. "Please, have a seat so we can pray."

Ben pulled out the chair at the head of the table—the place his father used to occupy before he'd died of a heart attack five years ago. Since that time, Ben had taken over running the farm, while trying to keep up with his own horseshoeing business. It was a lot of responsibility for a young single man, but Ben never complained and seemed content to live at home and help his mother. Dorothy wished she had more sons to share the load, or that her daughter, Lucinda, lived closer so that her husband, James, could help out. But they'd moved to Nappanee two years ago and didn't get to visit often.

"Are you sure you wouldn't like to go with me today?" Dorothy tapped Ben's arm. "It's been a while since you've gone anywhere."

"What do you mean? Every time I get a call to shoe a horse, I have to leave the farm."

"You're right. What I should have said is, it's been a while since you went anywhere just for fun."

His brows furrowed. "A visit with your friend Eileen might be fun for you, but I wouldn't have much to say to her. Besides, your trip sounds more like a woman's day out."

"I realize that, but we'll be going out to eat lunch at one of the restaurants in Topeka." She bumped his arm again. "You always enjoy eating out."

"Maybe some other time. This isn't a good day since I have four horses to shoe." He folded his hands. "Shall we pray?"

"Of course." When Dorothy bowed her head and began her silent prayer, she asked God to bless her son and give him the desires of his heart. He was a fine man and deserved all the happiness he could get. Perhaps someday it would include a wife, for Dorothy certainly didn't want her son to be alone after she died.

⌒

Topeka

"I wish you hadn't come to work this morning." Elma pressed her lips together, watching as her sister moved toward the counter with a bolt of material. Thelma's footsteps seemed to drag with each step she took on this warm, humid first Saturday of June.

Normally, Thelma wouldn't be working at the store today, but since Anna's last day was a week ago, Elma would have been on her own today, so Thelma insisted on helping out, just as she had every day this week.

Thelma planted her feet in a wide stance. "I was not about to sit on my front porch and watch customers come and go all day, knowing you were here all alone, trying to do a million things at once."

Elma chuckled, despite her concern. "That's a bit of an exaggeration, wouldn't you say?"

Thelma giggled. "Well, I'm sure you got my meaning."

"I did, and I hope you got my meaning, as well. I'm really surprised Joseph allowed you to come over here today."

Thelma pushed her shoulders back and lifted her chin. "My husband doesn't order me about. Besides, he got up at the crack of dawn to meet Delbert for a little fishing."

Elma's eyes narrowed. "So Joseph doesn't even know you're here. Is that how it is?"

"No, he doesn't, but I'm sure he wouldn't care." Thelma placed the material on the counter. "This is for Eileen Lehman. I believe it's the right shade of green, since she described it as sort of a pine color. She'll be in sometime this morning to get it."

"Oh? When did you talk to her?" Elma brushed her hand across the counter, clearing away several strands of thread.

"Yesterday. I ran into her at the grocery store. She said she'd be coming to the store and told me what kind of material she needed."

"Oh, I see. Guess that's a good enough reason for you to come to work today."

Thelma gave no reply as she skirted around the counter and took a seat on the stool.

Elma released a long, low sigh. *If my sister is determined to be here today, then I'll make sure she doesn't work too hard. She can sit on the stool and wait on customers like she did earlier this week.*

∽

As the morning wore on, Thelma began to wish she'd stayed home and rested. Even though there were no sales, the store had been full of customers since they first opened. The balls of Thelma's feet ached, and her toes pushed against her leather shoes. She'd been on her feet too long, walking back and forth with bolts of material left on the counter after cutting fabric for some of their customers. How good it would feel to be barefoot right now. *I'll be good as a summer rain once I'm home relaxing with my feet up for a while.*

Thelma yawned, twisting her neck from side to side. *I wonder how Joe and Dell are doing. Wish I could have gone fishing with them. It would be a lot more relaxing than sitting on this hard stool, waiting on customers all morning. I don't understand why my sister won't let me help with more things.*

She glanced at the bolt of material she'd set behind the counter. It was almost noon, but there'd been no sign of Eileen Lehman. *I wonder if she forgot.*

"Are you ready to take your lunch break now?" Elma stepped up next to Thelma.

"I guess so. Sure wish we were able to eat together so we could visit. Seems like we don't get to talk much these days."

Elma placed her hand on Thelma's shoulder. "I'm sorry. With me working long hours at the store, plus having chores at home to do by myself, I don't have much free time anymore."

"Which is why you need to hire someone to help here at the store. There's way too much work for one person to do, and with me only working a few hours each day, most of the responsibility falls on you."

Elma pushed a wayward strand of hair off her face. "It's all right. I'll manage."

"I'll talk to Joseph and see if he can come over in the evenings to help with some of your outside chores."

Elma shook her head. "No, it's okay. He has enough to do at your place. Besides, the two of you need time alone to catch up on your day, make plans for the boppli, and enjoy being husband and wife."

Thelma glanced toward the ceiling at a bee trying to find a way out. Their conversation was interrupted when Eileen and another Amish woman came into the store. She couldn't help noticing the pleats in the woman's skirt and wondered if she might be from Grabill. Although she'd never been to Grabill, Elma had heard the women there wore pleated dresses.

"I'm here for my material." Eileen smiled, her dimples deepening in her slightly wrinkled cheeks. Then she motioned to the dark-haired woman beside her. "This is my friend, Dorothy Wagler. We grew up together in Shipshewana, but now she lives in Grabill and has for a good many years." Eileen gestured to the twins. "Dorothy, I'd like you to meet Thelma Beechy, and her twin sister, Elma Hochstetler."

"It's nice to meet you both." Dorothy offered a pleasant smile as she shook Thelma's and Elma's hands. "Eileen filled me in on how you both acquired this store after your grandparents died."

"Jah." Elma nodded. "It's been a challenge, but things are shaping up here at the store. My grandparents' old house, on the other hand, is still a work in progress."

Dorothy laughed. "I understand. I've lived in my home for over thirty years and still don't have everything the way I'd like it to be. My son lives with me, and his hands are full, running his own business and trying to keep the farm going. So I try not to ask him to do anything around the house unless it's absolutely necessary or something I'm not able to do myself."

"Dorothy's husband, Ray, passed away a few years ago, so trying to keep up the place has become a challenge," Eileen interjected.

"I'm sorry for your loss." Elma placed her hand on Dorothy's arm.

"Danki. It was difficult at first, but Ben and I are managing."

"We'd like to stay and visit awhile, but we're meeting two other friends for lunch, so I'd best pay for my material and get going." Eileen placed her black purse on the counter. "How much do I owe, Thelma?"

"I put your invoice next to the plastic bag." Thelma handed it to her.

While Thelma took care of ringing up Eileen's purchase, Elma waited on another customer who'd been at the back of the store.

"It's been a pleasure to meet you both," Dorothy said when Eileen was ready to go and Elma rejoined them. "Perhaps the next time I get up this way, I'll drop by your store and say hello."

"Jah, please do." Thelma waved, and Elma walked the two ladies to the door.

⌒⌒

Elma was about to shut the door behind Eileen and her friend when Lizzie Yoder showed up.

Elma watched as Lizzie tied her horse to the hitching rail. "Are you needing more thread or material?" she asked when Lizzie stepped onto the porch.

Grinning, Lizzie shook her head. "Not today. I heard you were looking for part-time help at the store, and I'd like to apply for the job."

Elma's eyebrows lifted. "Have you had experience working in a store such as this?"

Lizzie's gray head moved quickly up and down. "I worked in a fabric store in LaGrange for a few months, and since I enjoy sewing, I think I'd be perfect for the job." Her voice lowered. "Besides, I'm living alone right now, and could certainly use some money coming in."

"You did say your brother was moving, but I thought a friend would be living with you and sharing expenses."

Lizzie's shoulders pulled inward as she released a heavy sigh. "It didn't work out. I'm on my own."

Elma slipped her arm around the older woman's ample waist, pulling her into a side hug. "Well, then, since you need a job, and I need an extra pair of hands around here, I have only two words to say: you're hired."

Lizzie's eyes brightened. "Can I begin today?"

"I don't see why not. Thelma's worked all morning, but it would be good if she could go home and rest. So you can take over for her the rest of the afternoon."

"Danki, Elma. Okay, then, if you'll show me what to do, I'll get right on it."

"Why don't you head to the room at the back of the store? I'll meet you there as soon as I tell Thelma she's free to go home."

"Okay. No problem." Lizzie's arms swung as she ambled off toward the back of the store.

"I just hired Lizzie to work here part-time." Elma grinned, joining Thelma at the counter again.

Thelma's chin jutted out. "I'm not sure that's such a good idea, Sister."

"Why not?" Elma's smile faded.

"You know as well as I do that Lizzie tends to be forgetful." Thelma spoke quietly with one hand cupped around her mouth. "She also talks too much, and at her age, I doubt she'll be able to keep up with all the work needing to be done here."

"She says she's had experience working in a fabric shop in LaGrange, so I'm sure she'll do fine." Elma placed her hands on Thelma's shoulders. "Lizzie is starting work right now, actually. So you're free to go home now and take it easy the rest of the day."

Thelma blinked. "Are you kidding me?"

"Course not. I can see the fatigue on your face, and do I need to remind you what the doctor said about making sure you get plenty of rest?"

Thelma leaned forward, elbows on the counter. "I may as well do as you say, because I'm sure I will not win this argument." She glanced toward the back of the store and whispered, "I only hope you didn't make a mistake hiring Lizzie."

Elma bit down on her bottom lip. *I hope not, either, because if I did, it will be difficult to tell poor Lizzie I don't need her help anymore.*

Chapter 6

LaGrange, Indiana

The *fisch* aren't bitin' so good today, are they?" Delbert set his pole aside and leaned back, clasping his hands behind his head.

Joseph grunted. "I wouldn't complain if I were you." He pointed at the cooler near Delbert's feet. "You've caught two more fish than I have."

"True, but you know what, Joe? Even if I didn't catch a single fish all day, I'd enjoy being here at the pond with my best friend, taking in all the sights, sounds, and smells of nature. There ain't nothing better, as the old saying goes."

"I know exactly what you mean." Joseph gestured to a line of beetles trundling along a rotten log. "Nature at its finest, *jah*?"

Delbert reached over and poked his friend's arm. "You enjoy watchin' a bunch of *keffer*?"

Joseph snickered. "Sure do. All kinds of bugs are interesting to watch."

"Personally, I'd rather look at a butterfly or dragonfly."

"Now you sound like my fraa and her *zwilling*. Just the other day when we had a picnic in our yard, the twins were having fun watching all the butterflies."

"I doubt they saw any big ones this early yet. The monarchs aren't usually seen till the later summer months."

"You sound like an expert on the subject." Joseph grinned. "Now I've learned something about you I didn't know before."

Delbert rolled his eyes. "Don't you remember when we were boys and I used to catch butterflies with a net so I could study them awhile before letting 'em go?"

"Oh, yeah, I forgot about that." Joseph removed his straw hat and fanned his face with the brim. "Seems so long ago. The biggest thing on my mind these days is making sure Thelma takes good care of herself as we anxiously await the arrival of our boppli."

"Are you *naerfich* about becoming a daed?"

"Jah, a little nervous. Never expected to get married, much less father any children." His forehead wrinkled. "Sure hope I'll be a good daed."

"Ah, you'll do fine. I know you can't compare the two, but look how good you take care of Ginger. You have a caring heart, and I know you'll be a great daed."

"Danki for giving me the vote of confidence."

Squinting against the sunlight streaming through the trees, Delbert swatted a mosquito that had landed on his arm. "Doesn't look promising for me to ever get married or have any kinner. Guess I'm too set in my ways for true romance to blossom."

Joseph gave Delbert's shoulder a squeeze. "Don't give up, my friend. The right woman's out there for you somewhere. Who knows, it could even be someone you've courted before."

Delbert's eyebrows rose as he cocked his head to one side. "Are you thinking of anyone in particular?"

With a wink, Joseph shrugged. "I'll let you figure it out."

Delbert pointed to the other side of the pond before reeling in his line. "Now there's a nice sight to see a woman and a boy fishing together."

Joseph looked in that direction. "Isn't that the widow Rachel Lambright and her son, Ryan?"

"Yep, I believe you're right." Delbert reached into his lunch-box cooler, removed two bottles of root beer, and held one out to Joseph. "Are ya thirsty?"

Joseph's eyes lit up. "Sounds good."

The two sat sipping their sodas while three young fellows walked by with their poles. The boys went a ways up from them and wasted no time getting their lines in the water.

Delbert watched in amazement as one of the boys reeled in a fish. "Did you see that, Joe? The boy got a big one right away."

Joseph cupped his hands around his mouth. "That's a keeper. Nice work!"

"Thanks," the boy called back. "This is my favorite spot for catching the good ones."

"I think he just caught your fish, Joe," Delbert teased.

Joseph bobbed his head. "Maybe we oughta try that location the next time we come here to fish."

"Jah, if someone doesn't beat us to it, that is."

Topeka

Thelma sat on the front porch of her home, hands clasped over her stomach as the wicker rocker moved steadily back and forth. She intended to do some mending while watching the birds eat at the feeders this morning, but her sewing basket still sat on the small table beside her. She couldn't help that her blue-skied mood had turned to gray. It was hard not to feel useless as she watched several cars, as well as horse and buggies, go up and down the driveway leading to the store up behind Elma's house.

Wish I could work there full-time again. Sure miss the connection with the customers. Now Lizzie gets to work there in my absence and visit with everyone who comes into the store. Thelma shifted slightly in her chair. *Seems at this stage in my life I need to pray for patience and learn to be content.*

Thelma rested her head comfortably for a moment, while soft breezes tickled her face. *I'm sure I won't miss it so much once the baby is born. Joseph and Elma are probably right: it's important for me to take it easy right now.*

Thelma smiled when she felt the baby kick. Oh, how she looked forward to becoming a mother.

Her gaze lowered when a wet tongue slurped her ankle. Joseph's golden retriever looked up at her with solemn brown eyes and whined.

"I know, Ginger, you're missing your master, too." She combed her fingers through the dog's silky hair. Quite often when Joseph went fishing, he took Ginger along for company. But not today. This morning he'd mentioned that he planned to make a couple of stops after he and Delbert went their separate ways and didn't want Ginger waiting in the open buggy for him. In addition to the hot sun beating down on the animal, she might jump out and try to follow him into one of the stores, like she'd done once before.

Thelma closed her eyes and leaned her head against the back of the rocker as she continued to rock.

Yip! Yip!

She stopped rocking, and her eyes snapped open. "Sorry, Ginger. I didn't mean to rock on your tail." Thelma checked the dog over to be sure she was all right.

Ginger was a good companion. Talking to the dog was better than sitting here all alone. *Maybe I'm dealing with those silly hormones other pregnant women have talked about.* She patted her stomach when the baby kicked again. *There's a miracle inside me, and I need to stop feeling sorry for myself. If anyone's to be pitied, it's my sister. She works so hard and lives all alone in that big old house without a word of complaint. Sure hope Elma didn't make a mistake hiring Lizzie to help out in the store. I wonder how things are going over there this afternoon.*

∽

Elma was relieved when things slowed down at the store after Thelma went home, because Lizzie wasn't working out quite as well as she'd hoped. In addition to moving about the store like a turtle carrying a load of bricks, the chatterbox spent too much time visiting with customers.

And I thought my sister was talkative. Lizzie could talk circles around Thelma. Elma sat on the stool behind the counter, pressing her fingers to her temples. *Maybe things will get better after she's worked here awhile. I can't expect her to do everything right on the first day. Sure hope that's how it goes, because Lizzie needs a job, and I certainly need help.*

Elma glanced at the clock on the wall across from her. One more hour and she'd be closing the store for the day. She looked forward to going to church tomorrow, and except for feeding the animals, it would be a day of rest. Most assuredly, she needed some time to let down. More than likely she'd spend Sunday afternoon with Thelma and Joseph. One more thing to look forward to.

"Yeow! *Iem schtachel!*"

Bee sting? Elma jumped off the stool and raced to the back of the store, where she found poor Lizzie wincing while holding her thumb. "When I picked up a bolt of material, I didn't notice the bee on it, until the pest stung me." She gave a slow, disbelieving shake of her head. "This has not been a good day for me. First, I dropped a box on my foot. Then I bruised my knee when I bumped into the step stool in the back room. And now this." Lizzie's face contorted. "I hope you don't think I'm accident prone."

"No, of course not." Elma moved closer to Lizzie. "Are you okay? You're not allergic to bee stings, I hope."

Lizzie shook her head. "Never have been before, and I've been stung plenty of times over the years. It hurts like crazy, but I'm sure I'll be fine."

"Let's go in the back room, and I'll get out the first-aid kit. I have a homeopathic remedy specifically for bee stings."

"Okay." Lizzie offered Elma a weak smile. "I hope there aren't any more *ieme* in the store. One nasty sting is enough for this old lady."

Elma's lip curled, remembering the bees she'd seen here a few weeks ago. She didn't want to risk having any customers getting stung and would need to find a way to keep the bees out of the store. It probably wouldn't hurt to take a look outside around the perimeter of the store to see if there were any bee nests. She wouldn't do it without bug spray, though. There might be a can in the back of the store, or for sure, underneath the kitchen sink at the house.

Maybe Delbert could take care of the problem by putting in new screens on the windows, and possibly adding a screen door at the front of the store. Elma tapped her chin. He'd been by earlier this week and put new flooring down in the bathroom. Before Delbert left, he'd told Elma to let him know if she needed anything else. *Think I'll give him a call this evening and see when he'd be free to come by again.*

Elma stepped into the back room behind Lizzie. "If you'll take a seat, I'll have a look at your thumb."

Grabill

"I hope you don't mind cold sandwiches tonight, Ben." Dorothy set a platter of lunch meat and cheese on the table. "I got back from Topeka later than expected and felt too mied to fix a big meal."

"It's fine, Mom. I'm tired myself, so a lighter meal is okay by me." Ben took a seat at the head of the table, and when he bowed his head, Dorothy did the same.

After they finished praying, she passed him the bread. "How'd your day go?"

"It was busy. After I got all my customers' horses shoed, I worked in the fields awhile and watered your garden."

Her cheekbones grew warm as she clasped his arm. "Danki. I meant to do it this morning, but my driver showed up, so I figured I'd have to do it when I got home."

"Now you don't have to worry about it at all." Ben helped himself to the meat and cheese then slathered his bread with mayonnaise.

"You're such a considerate son. Don't know what I'd do without you."

A flush crept across his face. "Now don't get all sentimental, Mom. I'm only doing what any good *sohn* would do for his mamm."

Dorothy handed him a bowl of strawberry gelatin. "You've made a lot of sacrifices for me since your daed's passing. A man your age ought to be married and starting his own family, instead of taking care of his old mother."

"First of all, you're not old." Ben's glass dripped with condensation as he took a drink. "And even if I had a fraa and kinner, I'd still see to your needs."

"I believe you would." Dorothy fiddled with her napkin, wondering how best to tell Ben the plans she'd made for tomorrow. He wouldn't like it if he thought she was trying to play matchmaker, but desperate times called for desperate measures.

"How come you're staring at your plate? Aren't you gonna eat, Mom?"

"Umm, jah. I was thinking, is all." She picked up a piece of bread.

"About what?" His voice muffled as he bit into his sandwich.

"About what I should fix for Sunday evening supper. Is there anything special you'd like to have?"

He lifted his broad shoulders. "Don't go to any trouble on my account. We hardly ever have a big meal on Sundays, unless we're having company."

"Well, actually. . ." Dorothy paused to make her sandwich.

"Actually, what, Mom?"

"I invited the Grabers to spend Sunday evening with us. Since they moved a few miles south, and are no longer in our church district, I thought it would be nice if we had some time to visit. I'm not sure what to fix for supper, though. What do you think about a roast with potatoes and carrots?"

Ben shrugged, popped the last of his sandwich into his mouth, and chewed. "I didn't realize you missed seeing them so much. As I recall, you and Paul's Ada were never that close."

"Maybe we're not close, but we do know each other, and. . ."

He slapped the table with his open hand, looking directly at her. "Oh, wait a minute. Think I'm beginning to understand. You invited the Grabers, hoping they'll bring their unmarried daughter along. Am I right?"

"Well. . ."

"Forget it, Mom. If it's meant for me to find a fraa, I'll do my own looking. So please don't try to match me up with Martha Graber." His forehead wrinkled. "Besides, she's ten years younger than me, not to mention we have nothing in common."

"Okay, but you need to keep an open mind."

Ben lifted his cup and sipped. "My mind is open, and I know you worry about me, Mom, but there's no need. I'm perfectly happy being single."

Dorothy wasn't sure about that, but if things didn't work out between Ben and Martha, she would keep looking. There had to be a young woman here in Grabill good enough for her son. Of course, it would have to be someone who was content to remain in Allen County, because this was Ben's home, and hers, too. If he should ever decide to move, Dorothy didn't know what she would do.

Chapter 7

Topeka

Y ou've been quiet all evening, Thelma. Is something bothering you?" Joseph asked after opening their bedroom window.

"No, not really." Thelma pulled the bedcovers aside, breathing in the moist night air. "I've been thinking about Elma."

"Is it about her being lonely or working too hard at the store?"

Thelma took a seat on the end of the bed and removed the pins holding her bun in place. "I'm concerned about both of those things, but just now I was thinking about Elma and Delbert."

Joseph took a seat beside her and combed his fingers through her long hair as it cascaded down her back. "What about her and Delbert?"

"He's been over at her place a lot lately." She smiled, leaning back and enjoying her husband's attention. "Wouldn't it be something if he and Elma got together after all?"

"I don't think it's likely to happen. Remember how things went between them when they courted before? Like when Delbert and I met you both at the pond to fish for the first time. Do you recall how Dell chose to sit in his favorite fishing chair and left your sister alone on the blanket she'd brought along to share?"

Thelma gave a slow nod.

"I remember the tension during that moment." Joseph raised his eyebrows. "It was awkward for me, and I'm certain it was for you, too."

"Jah, I admit, it was a little trying. Nonetheless, in the beginning of their relationship there was a definite attraction, and I'm sure my sister and Delbert were simply having a difficult time reading one another. Anyway, with the months that have passed since then, things could change."

Thelma sighed when Joseph picked up the brush she'd placed on the bed and began brushing her hair.

"Some things may have changed, but not necessarily them. Delbert's the same person he was two years ago, and so is your sister," Joseph reminded her.

"True, but I don't believe he'd go over there so often if he wasn't interested in her."

"Delbert's not paying social calls, Thelma. He's been doing work for Elma. A few days ago he put new screens in all the store windows, added a screen door, and took care of the bee problem."

"I realize that, but the more time they spend together, the better the chance for some little spark to be rekindled." Thelma tapped her chin while clicking her tongue. "Tomorrow's Saturday, and with the weather being so nice, I think we ought to have an evening barbecue."

"Sounds good to me. What kind of meat do you want me to cook?"

"I was thinking burgers, and we can invite Elma and Delbert to join us."

Joseph set the hairbrush down and reached over to clasp her hand. "Now don't get any ideas about playing matchmaker. If Dell and Elma are meant to be together, they don't need any help from either of us."

"I won't push, but they might need a little nudge."

He leaned over and kissed her cheek. "Let's forget about your twin sister and my best friend for now and concentrate on us."

Thelma slipped her hands around Joseph's neck and gave him a hug. "I love you, husband."

"I love you, too, my dear sweet wife."

⌒

When Elma opened the store Saturday morning, she was hit with a blast of warm air. For the latter part of June the weather had gotten quite hot, with high humidity making it hard to sleep even with the windows open at night. Last night, there'd been only a little breeze.

If Elma didn't get the store cooled off, any customers who came in would be miserable.

She hurried to open all the windows, thankful for the new screens Delbert had installed earlier in the week. She also made sure the front door was left open so whatever breeze might come up could blow through the new screen door, too. If it got too hot, Elma would turn on a few of the battery-operated fans she had for sale in the store. Stirring up the air would help a bit more. Elma was also relieved that she no longer had bees sneaking into the store and possibly stinging someone else.

She glanced out the window. No sign of Lizzie yet. *I hope she gets here before too many customers show up. She was late yesterday, too. Oh, dear, those potted flowers out there on the front porch are drooping. I'd better give them a drink of water.*

She pushed the screen door open and let it slap shut. There weren't any customers yet, so Elma got under way with the job at hand. She grabbed the coiled-up hose against the side of the store and added the nozzle to the end. Then Elma hauled the hose up the stairs, yanking on it when it became caught on one of the rungs. After twisting and yanking some more, she was able to free the hose. The tired old stairs creaked and moaned under her feet. There was quite a bit of rough wood showing that needed repair.

She frowned. *I'm not happy with these treads. I wish they were new and sturdy like the front porch of my house. Guess I'll need to add that to my list of things for Delbert to do.*

Elma began watering the flowers, when suddenly the water stopped. "Now what?" She twisted and turned the nozzle. Fearing something happened to the well pump, her gaze followed the hose's length down the steps. It was then she realized there was a crimp in the hose. "Well, at least it's not the pump." Elma breathed a sigh of relief as she unkinked the section that kept the water from flowing.

After the watering was done, Elma went back inside and gave herself a quick check. Looking down at her dark brown dress, she noticed a white cobweb clinging to the skirt. After brushing it away, she spotted a small spider crawling on her hand. "Yikes!" Elma slapped the bug off and stomped on it. "I hate *schpinne!*" she grumbled under her breath.

Elma moved about the store, making sure everything was in place, until she spotted a pile of debris near the back room, next to the broom and dustpan. Before leaving for home yesterday, Lizzie said she would sweep up the mess and dispose of it properly. She'd obviously forgotten.

Elma gritted her teeth. *She either forgot or got busy talking to someone, like she's done several times since I hired her to work here. I probably should speak to Lizzie about it, but I don't want to hurt her feelings. Besides, it's good to have a friendly relationship with our customers.*

Elma grabbed the dustpan and swept up the mess. *If you want something done, you may as well do it yourself. It's the quickest way to accomplish the task.* She groaned. *But then if I do all the work, what was the point in hiring Lizzie to help out in the store?*

It was almost nine thirty when Lizzie showed up. By then, five customers stood in line at the counter. Lizzie's plump cheeks colored like a bright red rose as she limped across the room. Elma noticed the elderly woman wore one black shoe and one sandal. Lizzie's swollen big toe poked out of the open-toed sandal.

"Oh, my! What happened to your toe?" Elma asked.

Lizzie moved toward the counter, wincing as she walked. "I dropped a jar of pickles on my foot last night, and my big toe took the brunt of it."

"How awful. It must hurt a lot."

Lizzie gave a nod. "It's not broken, though—only bruised. Had my driver take me to the hospital emergency room last night to have it checked out. The doctor said to stay off my feet as much as possible and put ice on the toe."

"You should have stayed home today and rested your foot." Elma spoke in a soothing tone.

"No way was I going to leave you in the lurch." Lizzie raised her dimpled hand.

Elma stepped down from the stool. "Well, then, you'd best sit here and wait on customers today, while I take care of other things."

Lizzie didn't have to be told twice. She made her way behind the counter and took a seat on the stool. Then she got down again. "Oops, I almost forgot." Lizzie pulled a small cushion out of her satchel. "I hope you don't mind, but I brought along something soft to sit on. In fact, you can keep it here for the counter stool. It'll be comfortable for Thelma, and you can sit on it, too."

"Good idea, Lizzie. Would you like to rub some Arnica on your toe?" Elma asked. "There's a tube of it in my first-aid kit. As you probably know, it's good for bruises and other injuries."

"Danki for your thoughtfulness."

"You're welcome." *Poor Lizzie,* Elma thought, as she hurried to the back of the store. *I hope coming here today won't be too much for her. Oh, I wish Thelma was free to work full-time again.*

⁓

By closing time, Elma was so tired she could barely put one foot in front of the other. While Lizzie waited on customers, she ran back and forth directing people to the items they wanted, cleaning up after anyone who dropped something on the floor, cutting material, and placing the bolts back on the shelf.

Elma was putting away the last bolt of material when she heard a deep droning noise coming from the front of the store. She set the fabric in place and hurried up front to investigate the sound. Halting her footsteps, her mouth dropped open. Lizzie was bent over, with her head on the counter. Her snores sounded like the reverberation of buggy wheels when some of the young Amish fellows got into a racing match.

Elma covered her mouth, stifling a snicker. Lizzie's fatigue wasn't what tickled her funny bone, though. It was the vibration of her snores against the wooden counter.

Sucking in a deep breath to rein in her emotions, Elma stepped around the counter and gave Lizzie's shoulders a gentle shake.

"*Was is letz do?*" Lizzie sat up with a start.

"Nothing's going on here." Elma spoke softly. "You nodded off, and I needed to wake you because it's time to close up the store and go home."

Lizzie leaned her head back and released a noisy yawn. "Oh, my, I must have been more tired than I thought." Glassy eyed, she glanced around. "Sure hope I didn't miss anyone wanting to pay for their items."

Elma shook her head. "Everyone's gone. I'm sure the last ones left before you fell asleep." *At least I hope that was the case.*

A horn tooted from outside, causing Elma to jump.

"I'll bet it's my driver. With my toe hurting so badly, I didn't want the bother of hitching my horse to the buggy this morning." Lizzie stepped off the stool and winced when her feet hit the floor. "I'm glad you let me sit up here most of the day. Don't think I'd have been able to do all the things you did today."

"Would you like me to go to the back room and get your empty lunch basket?"

Lizzie gave a quick nod. "I'd appreciate it."

As Elma headed back to get the basket, she thought about the cookout she'd been invited to at Thelma and Joseph's this evening. As tired as she was, she wouldn't be the best company, but at least it meant not having to cook a meal. If things went as they usually did whenever Thelma's husband fired up the barbecue grill, he would do all of the cooking. A little relaxation was what she needed.

ᴄ⁓

When Elma entered her sister and brother-in-law's backyard, she was surprised to see Delbert standing near the barbecue grill, talking to Joseph. Ginger rolled around in the grass nearby. When Thelma invited her to join them this evening she hadn't mentioned Delbert would be here.

As Elma approached, he looked over at her and smiled. "*Guder owed*, Elma. I didn't know you'd be here this evening. But then, guess I should have figured as much, since you live right across the street, not to mention being Thelma's twin sister."

Elma smiled in return. "Good evening, Delbert. I'm surprised to see you as well." She glanced around then looked at Joseph. "Is Thelma inside?"

"*Jah*. She'll be bringing out the paper plates and silverware, along with the potato salad she made."

"I'll go see if she needs any help." Elma gave the men a brief nod then hurried into the house. She found Thelma in the kitchen, putting paper plates, napkins, and plastic silverware on a serving tray.

Thelma smiled. "Oh, good, I'm glad you made it. I was afraid after working in the store all day you might be too tired to come over."

Elma shook her head. "I'm never too tired to spend time with you and Joseph."

"Delbert's here, too." Thelma took a bowl of potato salad from the refrigerator.

"I know. I spoke to him a few minutes before coming in here."

"I hope you don't mind that we invited him."

"Course not. It's your right to invite whomever you choose." Elma gestured to the tray. "Would you like me to carry it outside to the picnic table?"

"That'd be great. I'll bring the potato salad and condiments for the burgers on another tray."

"Maybe I should carry that one for you." Elma handed Thelma the silverware tray. "This is lighter and will be easier for you."

Thelma's brows furrowed as she pressed both hands against her hips. "I am perfectly capable of carrying the other tray. Besides, it's not that heavy."

"Okay, if you insist." Elma could see by the determined set of her sister's jaw that she was not going to give in. Thelma could be so stubborn sometimes.

"Is that a new dress you're wearing?"

"Jah. I've been eyeing the new color for a couple weeks at the store and finally decided to treat myself to a new dress." Elma gave a wide grin. "It's not my usual color choice, but I thought a change might be nice."

"That shade of lavender looks nice on you. You should wear it more often." Thelma's voice lowered. "I think Delbert's changed since we first met him, don't you?" She glanced out the kitchen window.

"Changed in what way?"

"He seems to be more even tempered."

"Maybe so. I hadn't really noticed."

Thelma turned to face her. "Maybe you should be more observant."

"What do you mean?"

"Oh, nothing." Thelma set the potato salad along with ketchup, mustard, mayonnaise, and pickles on the tray and picked it up. "Let's join the men. I think this is going to be a fun evening."

Elma wished she had her twin's enthusiasm. With Delbert here, she didn't feel like she could really be herself.

CHAPTER 8

Grabill

W here are you going?" Ben's mother asked when he started for the back door Saturday evening.

"Out to the barn to groom the horses," he called over his shoulder. "Think I'll wash 'em down before I start brushing."

"Sounds good. I'm sure the animals would enjoy a good bath." Mom sipped her coffee and set the mug in front of her. "But can you wait a few minutes before you go outside? I want to talk to you about something."

"Okay." Ben snatched his straw hat from the wall hook and turned back around. "What's up, Mom?"

"As you know, with this warm weather we've been having, my garden is doing quite well."

He gave a nod, pressing his back against the counter. "Jah, those cherry tomatoes and the Early Girls you're raising are mouthwatering. Their taste is far better than the ones they pick early and ship to the markets."

"True, and I'm thinking of taking some of my produce to the farmers' market in Shipshewana next month. Maybe the second Wednesday of July."

"Wouldn't you rather set up a fruit and vegetable stand in front of our place, like you've done in years past?"

Mom shook her head. "With the abundance of produce I have, I'd never get it all sold. By going to the market, I might be able to make some extra money to put aside for something I need later. Shipshewana brings in not only the locals, but a huge number of tourists as well."

"Good point. You might check with one of our drivers who owns a truck to see if they'd be available to take you that day." Ben shifted his weight. "Anything else?"

"Umm, jah—two things, actually."

He crossed his arms, waiting for her to continue while trying to remain patient. Sometimes Mom could be a bit long winded.

Ben thought about the customers he had to see this week. He wasn't sure until he verified his schedule, but it was getting closer to the time he'd be checking in on one of his biggest clients.

"Son, are you paying attention to me?" With arms crossed, Mom's foot tapped against the shiny linoleum floor.

"Sorry, Mom. I have a lot on my mind. Now what were you saying?"

"Well, first of all. . ." She stepped forward and stroked the side of his face. "It doesn't look like you've shaved today."

"I did it first thing this morning." He wiped a hand across his stubbly chin. "I can't help it that my beard grows faster than most men's."

"If you were married, you could let your beard grow, and it wouldn't be a problem."

Ben backed away, lifting his chin. "Please don't start with that again, Mom. If the good Lord wanted me to have a wife, she would look me right in the eye and say, 'Benjamin Wagler, you're the man I love and can't live without.'"

With a shake of her head, Mom snickered. "Not many women would be so bold."

"Exactly." He turned toward the door again and put on his hat. "Now if you don't need me for anything else, I'd better get out to the barn and take care of the *geil*."

"I do have one other quick question."

Ben paused, with his hand on the doorknob. "What is it?"

"When I take my produce to the farmers' market, would you like to go along?"

"It depends on whether I have any horses to put shoes on that day."

"Can't you make sure not to schedule any? I could use some help setting up my stand, and maybe during the sale things will go well, and I'll get a lot of business."

"Okay, but if I'm not free that day, you'd better see if someone else is free to go with you."

Mom gave him a wide smile then pointed to the door. "Better not keep those horses waiting."

"You're right. I'm on my way."

⁓

When Ben went outside, Dorothy got out a notebook and pen then took a seat at the kitchen table to make a list of all the garden produce she wanted to take to the farmers' market. She had peas and beans aplenty, as well as onions, zucchini, and tomatoes. In a few more weeks, carrots, cucumbers, and maybe some beets would also be ready.

Maybe I should also pick some of my colorful flowers to sell. Surely there would be some people attending the market who might be interested in buying a lovely bouquet.

Dorothy smiled, thinking about the fuss Martha Graber had made over her flowers when she'd been here last Sunday for supper with her folks. Martha especially admired the zinnias. Dorothy couldn't blame her. Zinnias were one of her favorite flowers, too. Bunched together in the flower bed, their rainbow of color was not to be missed.

Martha was as stunning as those flowers. A beautiful young woman such as her, with hair the color of straw and eyes as blue as the summer sky, would make any man stop and take notice. *How could my son not be interested in someone as lovely as her?*

Dorothy tapped the end of her pen along her jaw. *I need to have Martha over again, only this time without her parents. After supper I'll discreetly retire to my room, leaving Ben and Martha alone to visit. If they spend enough time together, surely they'll find some things they have in common.* She set the pen down and poured herself a cup of coffee. *My son's too timid for his own good. He needs to be more assertive around women.*

⁓

Ben finished washing his buggy horse, Fella, and led him back to the stall. Once inside, he grabbed the currycomb to untangle the animal's mane and tail. As Ben worked the comb slowly and carefully through Fella's hair, he couldn't help thinking about what his mom had said earlier. *"If you were married, you could let your beard grow, and it wouldn't be a problem."*

Ben sucked in a breath. *I understand why Mom wants me to find a wife, but she's trying to match me up with who she thinks is the right woman for me.* His shoulders slumped. It had been awkward the other evening when the Grabers came for supper. It was especially uncomfortable having Martha sitting across from him, and not finding much in common to talk about. *Mom means well, but I'm old enough to make my own decisions. I might decide to stay single, if that's what I choose to do with my life.*

Ben switched from the comb and used the soft-bristled brush, working it along the horse's side, while Fella munched on his hay. The sweet grassy aroma filled the air, tickling Ben's nose. The barn was quiet and peaceful—a nice area to think—just him and the horses.

Mom's buggy horse, Patsy, chewed on the hay in her stall across from them. Ben had taken care of her earlier. Patsy possessed a mild demeanor, which Dad had said he felt from the moment he'd purchased her at an auction. He brought her home for Mom so she would have an easygoing horse.

Ben preferred to take Fella out with his buggy, and sometimes he rode horseback. In addition to having more get-up-and-go, the horse always brought Ben numerous compliments. Even strangers commented on the animal's shiny, deep chestnut color. It was hard not to feel prideful.

Stepping away from Fella, Ben admired his work. All the brushing he'd done brought out a nice sheen to the horse's stunning coat. "Fella, you look good enough to take out on the town." He carried the brush and comb out of the stall and put them away. Then he went outside to where he'd given the horses their baths and returned the sponges to the shelf in the barn. Following that, Ben began coiling up the hose. When he backed up, he tripped over the bucket. Soapy water splashed out, soaking Ben's pant legs. "Oh, great!" He glanced toward the house and saw Mom looking out the window, shaking her head. *She probably thinks I'm a clumsy* dummkopp.

Heat flooded Ben's face as he retrieved the bucket and hurried back to the barn.

Topeka

"Those were some mighty good burgers, Joe. I couldn't stop at two, so I had to have three." Delbert laced his fingers together and placed his hands behind his head. "My compliments to the cook."

Joseph's face flushed a bit. "It doesn't take much to grill burgers. The real compliment should go to my fraa for her tangy potato salad. But I'm glad you enjoyed eating the meat." He paused and smiled at Thelma.

Delbert smacked his lips. "You're right. The salad was *appenditlich*. I had to have a second helping, in fact." He grinned at Thelma. "If I could find a single woman who made potato salad this good, I'd marry her tomorrow."

With little thought of what she was about to say, Thelma pointed to Elma. "My sister makes potato salad every bit as delicious as mine."

Elma's face flushed a deep crimson, while Delbert's ears turned bright pink.

Hoping to cover her slip of the tongue, Thelma changed the subject. "How did things go at the store today, Elma?"

"They were hectic, since Lizzie couldn't do any more than sit on the stool and wait on customers."

"How come? Doesn't she usually help with other things?" The question came from Joseph.

"Normally, she does, but Lizzie came to work today with a badly bruised big toe. She could barely walk, so I had no choice but to let her sit behind the counter, which meant I was on my feet most of the day. She did bring a cushion for the stool, which she said we could keep there."

"How'd she hurt her toe?" Thelma reached for her glass of iced tea, rubbing her fingers where moisture collected.

"She dropped a jar of *bickels* on it. Lizzie thought at first it might be broken, but the doctor said it was only a bad bruise." Elma sighed heavily. "I hate to say this, but Lizzie seems prone to accidents."

"That's not all." Thelma shook her head. "When I was helping at the store yesterday, I couldn't help noticing how forgetful Lizzie seemed to be. She was also quite the chatterbox with customers."

Delbert leaned forward, resting his elbows on his knees. "Sounds to me like her name oughta be 'Dizzy Lizzie.'" He chuckled and so did Joseph. Even Thelma had to hide a snicker behind her hand.

A slight muscle jumped in Elma's left cheek. "Better not say anything like that in front of poor Lizzie. She may have a few quirks, but she's really a dear soul."

"Maybe so, but from what I saw while installing new screens, that 'dear soul' is more of a hindrance than a help, Elma. If I were you, I'd look for someone more dependable to work in the store."

Elma's lips pressed together as her face tightened. "I appreciate your concern, Delbert, but as long as I'm in charge of the store, I'll decide who stays and who goes."

A sheen of sweat erupted on Delbert's forehead as he lifted his hands as if in surrender. "Okay, okay. . .no need to get all *umgerennt*."

"I am not upset." Elma folded her arms and looked the other way.

Thelma sagged in her chair, pressing a hand against her stomach. *Maybe I was wrong thinking Elma and Delbert might get together. It seems the problem between them from before is still there. If they could just learn to agree to disagree, things might go better. Well, I'm not giving up yet. Perhaps I'll try again some other time when Elma isn't so tired.*

CHAPTER 9

Since the store was usually closed on Mondays, Elma used this time to get caught up on things around the house and run errands. She had her lists on the kitchen table, where she'd been jotting down a few late additions.

Elma brewed some black tea and sat nibbling on blueberries that had come from her garden. "Yum. These berries are sure tasty." She added a dollop of vanilla yogurt and smacked her lips.

Tiger sat in a sunny spot on the floor not far from her. He seemed content, although he blinked his eyes against the intense light.

"I wish you could do some chores for me, Tiger. How about going out to the barn and getting the horse ready for me this morning?" Elma chuckled.

Tiger meowed; then his tongue came out as he began grooming himself. When he finished his bath, he plopped down and closed his eyes.

Elma picked up her dishes and went to the sink. She still needed to get her horse, Pearl, ready in the barn, but she needed to finish up in the kitchen first.

It would be nice if Thelma could come with me today. I'd welcome her company, and maybe she could drive Pearl while I jot down more items to my lists. Elma rinsed the blueberry juice from the bowl. *I miss the quality time we used to share.*

Today, being the last Monday in June, she'd decided to make a run to town for groceries and a few other items. One of the things she wanted to do was look for baskets she could use to display her garden produce when she went to the farmers' market next month. This would be Elma's first time renting a stand at the market, and she hoped it would be a profitable day.

In addition to selling her garden produce, Elma planned to take a few handmade items, along with flyers listing some of the things sold in the store and giving directions on how to get there. While most of the locals knew about Elma and Thelma's store, many tourists did not. So her trip to Shipshewana the second Wednesday of July would have a twofold purpose.

Joseph would take time from his harness shop that day to accompany Elma and Thelma to the market. Of course, they'd have to close the store. Elma certainly couldn't expect Lizzie to manage by herself. Thelma had agreed, saying it would be less to worry about having the store closed for the day. There were times, like the day Lizzie had come to work with a bruised toe, when the poor woman could barely function. Expecting Lizzie to run the store by herself would be asking for trouble.

Elma had already taken the buggy out of the shed in readiness for her trip to town, so she placed her purse inside on the seat and headed for the barn to get Pearl. Stepping through the tall double doors and into the building, she heard the rustle of hay and smelled nose-tickling straw, but didn't hear her horse's usual whinny-greeting or hooves scuffing the wooden floor.

The old boards creaked as she made her way over to Pearl's stall. The gate whined when she opened it and stepped inside. Pearl stood with her backside near the wall, almost as if she was leaning against it for support.

"What's the matter, girl? Are you mad at me for not putting you in the pasture this morning so you could run and kick up your heels?" Elma ran a currycomb over the curve of the mare's back. "Well, I had a good reason. I need you to take me to town."

Pearl nickered, nuzzling Elma's hand.

Elma smiled. She loved this old horse, and felt ever so thankful Dad had brought her to them a few years ago, when he and Mom came for a visit. Pearl was gentle and reliable—nothing like Rusty, the unpredictable horse they'd inherited from their grandfather when he and Grandma died, leaving them the house and store. Rusty was spirited and could be a handful at times.

Elma was glad Thelma had taken Rusty as her horse when she'd married Joseph. From the start, she'd been able to control him better than Elma could. Elma figured Rusty rightly sensed her fear. Merely thinking about the feisty gelding made her break out in a cold sweat.

Elma put Pearl's lead rope in place to take her from the stall, but the horse only snorted with huffing breaths and wouldn't budge.

"Come on, girl, now don't you be stubborn this morning." Elma gave a tug.

Pearl took a few faltering steps and halted. The horse seemed to be favoring her right back leg, appearing not to put any weight on it.

"What's the matter, Pearl?" Elma looked down, and she gasped when she saw a nasty gash on the horse's back leg. "Ach, you poor thing. No wonder you don't want to go anywhere with me."

Elma removed Pearl's leade rope and was quick to close the stall door. She'd need to call the vet immediately. Hopefully he would be free to come out right away.

$$\sim$$

Thelma hummed as she stood at the counter near the kitchen sink, preparing a pot of garden mint tea. Their bishop's wife, Lena Chupp, would be here soon, bringing some baby items one of her grandchildren had outgrown. Thelma looked forward to going through them to see what she might be able to use. It had been a while since she'd visited with Lena, so she'd invited her to stay and have lunch.

A knock sounded on the back door. Thinking it must be Lena, Thelma hurried to answer. Opening the door wide, she stepped back in surprise. Her red-faced sister stood on the porch, blowing out a series of short breaths. Elma's stooped posture and wrinkled forehead let Thelma know she was distressed about something.

"Elma, what's wrong? You look umgerennt."

"I am very upset." Elma stepped inside. "Pearl's been hurt, and she won't be able to pull my buggy for several weeks."

"Ach, my! What happened? Have you called the vet?" Thelma's body tensed.

"Pearl has a gash on her right back leg. I'm not sure when she got the cut, but I called Dr. Brown as soon as I discovered it, and he came to check Pearl right away." She paused, her chin trembling a bit. "At first we didn't know how it had happened, but then the vet discovered a nail sticking out of one of the lower stall boards. Don't know why I didn't see it before."

"Is your *gaul* going to be all right?" Thelma's concern escalated. *If Pearl dies, Elma will be devastated. I'd miss that trusty old horse, too. And then she would need to buy another buggy horse, which would be expensive.*

"Dr. Brown put medicine on the wound, wrapped it good, and gave her an antibiotic. His instructions were to keep an eye on her and watch for infection. I'll need to change her bandage once a day and apply the ointment to the gash." Tears gathered in Elma's eyes, and she blinked several times. "I hope I can do a good job for her. The doctor left medicine for Pearl, and bandages to rewrap the wound, but I'll need to pick up more sterile pads in town. I hate to say this, but if my horse doesn't recover well enough, she may not be able to pull the buggy anymore."

Thelma slipped her arms around Elma and patted her back. "Hang in there and try not to worry. I'm sure she'll be fine."

"I hope so, but in the meantime, I'll either have to ride my bike everywhere or rely on a driver to take me places. Also, I wouldn't mind some support, or at least having someone next to me while I change Pearl's bandage tomorrow. Do you think you or Joseph could come over to help?"

"Not to worry. One of us will be there. Oh, and you can borrow one of our horses until Pearl is better." Thelma gave her sister a hug.

"Danki." Elma smiled, returning the embrace. "I appreciate it. As a matter of fact, I was planning to go into town today to do some shopping, so can I borrow Joe's horse? In addition to the sterile pads for Pearl, I need groceries, plus I want to buy several baskets to display the produce I'll be taking to the farmers' market in a few weeks."

"Rusty is available, but Joseph's already left for work, so his horse isn't here this morning."

Elma's eyes widened as she pressed her hands to the sides of her head. "Oh, no, I can't take Rusty. That horse is too temperamental for me."

"Both Joseph and I have worked with him over the last two years, and he's more manageable than he was before."

Elma moved closer to Thelma. "Could you go with me today? You've always handled Rusty better than me."

"I would if I could, but Lena Chupp will be here soon, and I invited her to join me for lunch, so she'll probably stay awhile."

Elma's shoulders slumped. "Maybe I'll see if one of our drivers is available."

Thelma clasped her sister's arm. "You should take Rusty today. You need to get past your fear."

"I can't." Elma's chin trembled. "Even the thought of taking that horse makes me naerfich."

"I understand your nervousness, but as I said before, Rusty is easier to handle now."

"For you maybe, but I doubt he would be for me."

"Just keep a firm hand on the reins and let him know who's boss. I'm sure he will do fine for you."

Elma's shoulders curled forward as she clutched her arms to her chest. "Okay, I'll give Rusty a try, but if things don't go well, I will never use him again."

Thelma glanced at the clock. "Lena won't be here for another fifteen minutes, so I'll go outside with you and hitch Rusty to the buggy."

⌒

Elma's fingers ached as she clung to the reins. Other than tossing his head a few times, so far Rusty had behaved himself. Maybe the trip into town wouldn't be so bad after all.

She loosened her grip a bit and tried to relax. Rusty must have sensed it, for he stopped shaking his head. The closer Elma got to town, the more her senses heightened. The car traffic grew heavier, and some drivers got a little too close for comfort. She wondered if all this was worth putting herself through so much stress. Her thoughts raced. *What if something spooks or upsets Rusty? If he takes off and won't slow down, I'll be in a pickle.*

Elma could tell by the sweat rolling down her back that she was losing faith in her abilities. She spotted a place to pull off the road to rest and collect her thoughts for a moment. As she sat holding the reins, Elma closed her eyes to pray. *Lord, allow me the strength and safety to continue on with this day You have made. Please surround me with Your wonderful peace and help me not to be afraid. Amen.*

After a while, Elma's nerves calmed as she allowed the horse to take the lead. With all his years of experience pulling the buggy for her grandparents, Rusty certainly knew the way to town.

Elma waved to an English neighbor on a riding lawn mower, cutting his grass. She'd seen it before but still had to giggle, watching the barn swallows swoop at bugs the mower kicked up.

They'd almost made it to the first intersection in town when a car pulled out of a side street without stopping, right in front of the horse and buggy. Rusty planted his hooves, halting the buggy, before Elma could even pull back on the reins.

She blinked a couple of times. *Thank You, Lord. What an answer to prayer.* Leaning forward, she clucked to the horse. "Good boy, Rusty. You are one schmaert horse and may have just saved our lives."

Elma jumped when the driver blared his horn at her and was even more stunned when the car kept going. *How can people be so rude?*

Despite the prickling of her scalp, Elma drew a deep breath and continued in the direction of town. Rusty nickered as if to assure her that he had everything under control. If she needed to go any distance in the next few weeks, perhaps she would borrow Thelma's horse again.

CHAPTER 10

Shipshewana, Indiana

Entering the farmers' market, Elma's gaze came to rest on the rows of tables with bright tablecloths, filled with local seasonable produce. Many craft tables were filled with various handmade items, and food vendors were selling cookies, breads, pies, and beverages. One English man pulled his red pickup truck into one of the open spots to sell his rustic birdhouses. Cloth awnings of different colors hung behind several of the booths. While other tables sat outside her view—where numerous miscellaneous items were sold—unless Thelma and Joseph stayed at the table, it wasn't likely Elma would get to check out many of the vendors' tables.

Even though the market hadn't opened yet, an increasing number of visitors already were milling about. The aroma of fresh herbs and ripening berries mingling with fragrances from homemade soaps and creams filled Elma's senses as she drew a deep breath. She appreciated being able to take part in a rural event that nurtured the feeling of community spirit.

"Look at all the people who came to sell their wares at the market today," Joseph commented as he helped Elma set up her table. Thelma had brought a few things to sell, too, but most of the proceeds from whatever they sold would go to pay for more repairs needing to be made at the house or store.

Elma inhaled sharply. It seemed the list of repairs at both places was endless. Thelma and Joseph were fortunate to have bought a place in such good shape.

Now don't start feeling sorry for yourself. Elma picked up one of the baskets she'd bought a couple of weeks ago and filled it with fresh fruits and berries. She put cucumbers, beets, peppers, and carrots in another basket and a mixture of both in a third basket. Soon, all the baskets were full, and several other items were placed on the table by themselves.

"The display looks nice." Thelma gestured to a hefty water-melon. "It's a warm day, so I'm sure lots of people will be looking for sweet-tasting summertime fruit such as this."

"I hope so. Sure don't want to haul a lot of this produce home at the end of the day and then try to figure out how we're going to eat all of it."

"Not to worry." Joseph motioned to the table. "If I were a betting man, I'd bet most of your produce will be gone by the day's end."

Thelma nodded. "I believe my husband is right."

"Well, it remains to be seen." Elma rummaged through the over-sized bag she'd brought along and retrieved some chair pads she'd remembered to bring for the day. She picked out a bottle of sunscreen and set it aside for later. "It's good to be prepared and as comfortable as we can. Lizzie gave me this idea." Holding up the cushions, she placed them on the hard, wooden stools they'd also brought from home and took a seat. Thelma sat on the other stool. "My only con-cern," Elma admitted, "is all the other vendors with the same type of produce as mine. It may be too much competition."

⌒

"I'm glad you came with me this morning." Smiling, Dorothy looked up at her son. "If things get really busy, I'll need your help at my table."

"No problem, Mom. That's why I agreed to come along." Ben glanced around. "Looks like there's a lot of other tables full of pro-duce, though. Sure hope you're able to sell most of your things."

"I hope so, too, but if not, at least I can say I tried." Dorothy placed a dark green tablecloth on the table and began setting things out.

Ben grabbed a box filled with a variety of plants Dorothy had brought to sell. "I don't see too many people selling flowers like yours, so that should help."

"Jah. Providing anyone who comes to the market today is looking for flowers." She folded her arms. "I was excited about coming here, but now a few doubts are settling in."

Ben put his hand on her shoulder. "Don't worry, Mom. Things will go okay. Just try to relax and enjoy the day."

"You're right." She smiled. "I need to keep a positive attitude."

"Good to hear." Ben set the last of her things in place. "Would ya mind if I take a look around before the market opens for business? If things get busy later on, I may not have a chance to do it."

"Go right ahead. I'll be here waiting when you get back."

"I won't be gone long," Ben called over his shoulder as he headed off.

⟋⟍

Ben wandered around for a bit, savoring the tantalizing smells of the food vendors. He and Mom had eaten a hearty breakfast this morning, but the thought of chomping down on a juicy hot dog or bag of tasty kettle corn made his stomach growl. Well, he'd have a chance to do that later on, when it was time for lunch. For now, though, he wanted to see what some of the vendors were selling, because he might not get the opportunity again. It would be great looking around with fresh inventory sitting undisturbed at the different booths. Having first pick of things made it worth getting here early.

Ben stopped to admire some knives on display at a nearby booth. He picked one up and let it rest in his hand, feeling its weightiness. He couldn't resist running his thumb along the handle where the detailed carving of an eagle was made. *I'm glad my mamm convinced me to come and help her today. Maybe she'll sell enough produce at the market to make it worth her while.*

"What do you think about that knife there?" the bearded English vendor asked.

"It's nice. I have a few at home, but none like this one." Ben placed it on the table in front of him.

"I've collected many through the years, and passed a lot of them down to my sons."

"I'm sure they liked receiving knives like these." Ben glanced at an enclosed case next to him. "Think I'll take this one off your hands."

He pointed to his choice and reached for his wallet.

"Okay." The vendor took Ben's cash and put the knife in its original box then handed it to him.

"Thanks." Ben carried his purchase along while he checked out a few more tables. The smell of food cooking filled the air, and the irresistible aroma made his mouth water. Fighting the urge to get something to eat, he headed back to their table.

His mother smiled at him. "I see you found something to buy already. What did you get?"

Ben passed the box to her. "Found a nice knife to add to my growing collection."

"That is a nice one." She touched the handle. "Your daed liked to collect coins, as you well know. He had socks with money in them inside his dresser, and little boxes containing collector coins. Of course, he ordered more the older he got. If a coin caught his eye, he'd try to get it." Her eyes misted.

Ben's mom became sentimental when it came to his dad. For that matter, so did Ben. *Bet Dad would have enjoyed being here today, and he would've gotten Mom to wander around with him to check out all the wares.* Ben winced. *They were so close. What a shame he's no longer with us.* It seemed to be getting a little easier for himself, but Ben could only imagine how difficult it had been for Mom to lose her spouse.

Ben left the knife with his mother and wandered up and down a few more aisles, checking out everything from books, household tools, straw hats, to lots of collectable things. Nothing caught his interest, until he spotted a produce stand where a young Amish woman stood placing fruits and vegetables in baskets. Thinking it might be good to check out the competition, he headed that way.

⁓

"Since we're all set up, would you mind if Joseph and I walked around for a bit?" Thelma leaned close to Elma. "If things get busy at the stand later on, this may be our only chance to look at some of the other tables and booths."

"Go right ahead. If people start coming in before you get back, I'm sure I can manage." Elma gestured to the basket closest to her.

"Before you leave, do you think this one looks okay, or should I add a few more pieces of fruit?"

"Looks good enough to eat." Joseph chuckled. "Not the basket—just what's inside."

Elma smiled. "You two go on, now, and enjoy yourselves."

"Okay. We shouldn't be gone too long." Thelma waved and headed off with Joseph in the direction of the booths selling food.

Elma snickered. No doubt her sister had a craving for something. Thelma had confided in Elma on the drive here this morning that two nights ago she'd gotten up in the wee hours to eat a couple of brownies. Thelma needed to eat something healthier than chocolate, especially late at night. She might have ended up with heartburn, and with her being pregnant, it would be even more miserable. Elma would look through her natural desserts cookbook for a better treat to bake for her twin.

Elma took her notepad from the tote she'd brought along and jotted down a reminder. *Since Thelma craves sweets, my recipes will fill the void yet won't be bad for her. My sister has a habit of eating whatever she wants, but not always what is good for her.*

I'll probably never know what it's like to have pregnancy cravings, Elma mused. *But if I ever do, I hope it's not for sugary treats. I'll be sure to eat well, avoiding temptations, and give my unborn child the best start I possibly can.*

Elma had always been the more health conscious of the twins, although she did sometimes splurge—especially when it came to certain desserts. She'd walk a mile through the pouring rain for a piece of homemade cherry pie.

Elma smiled when a few children ran past, giggling while they gave chase to each other. She noticed some other kids sat with parents behind tables, watching with an I-want-to-play-too look in their eyes.

Oh, to be young again. Elma heaved a sigh, wishing there was a way to slow life down a bit. It seemed like yesterday she and Thelma were eager children.

Elma's thoughts drifted in another direction as she reflected on how things had been going at home, as well as inside the store. While Lizzie was not the best helper she'd ever had, having her working in the store was better than no help at all during the times Thelma couldn't be there. Lizzie kept her company, and with busy times in the store, the workdays flew by. Besides, Lizzie needed a job, and Elma didn't have the heart to let her go. It made her feel good to help the woman out, even though Elma worked like two people at times, and at lightning speed to keep up with everything.

With the exception of Tiger being a pest much of the time, things were going okay at the house. Of course, Elma still spent many hours by herself and struggled with loneliness, but it was a comfort to have her twin sister living across the street. Looking over there and seeing activity made being alone a little more tolerable. It was nice to know she could pop over from time to time if the loneliness became too unbearable.

"Looks like you have some nice produce here."

Elma jerked at the sound of a deep voice. When she looked up, a pair of brilliant blue eyes stared at her. It was difficult not to gaze back at them.

"Sorry if I startled you." The Amish man's deep-dimpled smile seemed sincere.

"It's okay. I was deep in thought when you stepped up to my table." Elma couldn't help but notice that he wasn't sporting a beard.

"I was admiring your produce and the way it's displayed." Leaning forward, he reached out to pick up an apple, but in the process, he bumped the table. The next thing Elma saw was a blur of red fruit leaving as the basket toppled over and everything spilled out. Some of the produce rolled off and under the table.

"Sorry about that." A blotch of red erupted on the man's face as he bent down and crawled under the table to retrieve the items from the upset basket. At the same time, Elma went under from her side of the table. They both reached for an apple, and their hands touched.

Elma jerked her head, bumping it on the underside of the table. "Ouch!"

"Are you okay?"

"Jah, I'm fine." Elma picked up the apple, backed out, and clambered to her feet just as her twin sister stepped up to the table.

Pursing her lips, Thelma glanced at Elma, then at the man who had been under the table but now stood facing them. Arms folded, she tilted her head, looking back at Elma. "What's going on here, Sister?"

CHAPTER 11

Elma's hand trembled as she gathered up the rest of the apples and placed them on the table. Between her sister's disapproving look and the Amish man's curious stare, she couldn't seem to find her voice and could hardly look her twin in the face.

Thelma nudged Elma's arm. "What's going on? How come the produce is in such disarray?"

Before Elma could respond, the man raised his hand and spoke. "It's my fault. I reached out for a piece of fruit and knocked the basket over." He picked up a few more items and placed them in the basket.

Joseph joined them at the table, squinting at the Amish man. "You look familiar to me. Have we met before?"

"I'm not sure. My name is Benjamin Wagler, and I live in Grabill." He swiped a hand across his forehead, pushing a chunk of his thick brown hair under the brim of his straw hat. "Most folks just call me Ben."

Joseph pulled his fingers through the ends of his beard; then a slow smile spread across his face. "I know where I've met you. A few years ago I was near Grabill, looking at some used harness-making equipment. The fellow who owned the farm was Abe Miller, and you were there, shoeing his horses."

Ben nodded. "That's right; I shoe horses for a living, and Abe's still one of my steady customers."

"I'm Joseph Beechy. This is my wife, Thelma, and her twin sister, Elma Hochstetler."

"It's nice to meet you," the twins said in unison while Ben shook Joseph's hand.

Ben shifted his gaze from Thelma to Elma. "You two certainly look alike. In fact, if it weren't for. . ." His face colored as he glanced at Thelma's baby bump then looked quickly away.

"People have been getting us mixed up since we were *bopplin*." Thelma chuckled. "Of course now, and for a while yet, it'll be easier to tell us apart."

Ben gave a brief nod. "Is this your produce stand, Elma? Or are you running it with a husband or some other family member?"

Elma's cheeks burned hot. Was Ben only curious, or could his question have been asked to find out if she was married?

She cleared her throat, hoping she could speak without stumbling over the words. With the exception of Delbert, it had been some time since she'd met an Amish man as attractive as Ben.

"Oh, my sister's not married," Thelma blurted before Elma could respond.

The heat Elma felt on her face radiated to her neck, chest, and arms. She tried to gather her thoughts before saying something foolish. "Umm. . .most of the produce on the table is mine, but some of the vegetables and fruit are from Thelma's garden."

"My mamm has a table, too. She's selling some flowers in addition to produce from our yard." Ben gestured toward the area near the front entrance of the farmers' market.

"There seems to be lots of folks selling fresh produce today." Joseph bent down and picked up several radishes that had fallen on the ground during the mishap.

"Do you live here in Shipshewana?" Ben looked at Elma.

She shook her head. "We live in Topeka, and my sister and I run a general store."

"Well, mostly you run the store these days," Thelma put in. "I only work a few hours, a couple days a week anymore."

"It must be difficult to run the store by yourself when your sister's not working." Ben kept his focus on Elma.

"Things can get hectic," she admitted, "but I have a woman who helps out when Thelma's not there."

"When Joe and I were walking around, we stopped at one of the stands selling homemade pies and flavored coffees." Thelma placed her hand on Elma's arm. "I think I spotted cherry pie there. I know it's one of your favorites." She gave her sister a playful wink. "Why don't you go over and sample some?"

"Oh, I can't. The market will be open for business soon, and I wouldn't want to miss any prospective customers."

"Don't worry about that." Joseph put a few more pieces of fruit back on the table. "Thelma and I will watch the table. Besides, my fraa could use some shade and rest on one of these stools." He motioned for his wife to take a seat.

Shifting her weight, Elma bit her lip. "I suppose I could go check it out, but I won't be gone long."

"Would you mind if I tag along?" Ben asked. "I could use a cup of coffee, and a slice of pie sounds good, too."

"Okay, that's fine with me." What else could she say? It surprised Elma when he said he wanted to go along, and it would be rude to say she preferred to go alone. Besides, she might enjoy his company.

⌒

Ben didn't normally feel a connection to a woman he'd only just met, but after visiting with Elma a short time, he felt as if he'd known her awhile. They'd been sitting on a bench, drinking coffee and eating pie for half an hour or so, and he wished it could be longer. Elma was not only intelligent and interesting to talk to, but her pleasant smile captivated him.

"Have you ever visited Grabill?" he asked.

She shook her head. "Between the store and keeping things going at my house, I don't have a lot of free time to explore other towns in the area."

"It's a small community, but it's where I grew up, so I feel comfortable there." Ben drank the last of his coffee. "How about you? Have you lived in Topeka all your life?"

"No, Thelma and I were raised in Sullivan, Illinois." She blotted her nicely shaped lips with a napkin.

"So how'd you end up here?"

Ben listened intently as Elma explained how she and her twin sister had inherited their grandparents' home, as well as their store. "I assume Thelma wasn't married to Joseph back then?"

"No. She met him not long after we moved here."

Ben was tempted to ask if Elma was being courted by anyone but thought better of it. She might think he was too forward. Since they'd both finished their pie and had places they needed to go, he rose to his feet and tossed his paper plate and cup into the nearest trash can. When Elma stood, he politely threw hers away, too. "Sometime, when I'm up this way again, maybe I'll stop by your store and say hello."

She smiled. "That would be nice. The name of our store is E&T's General Store, and it's on Meadowbrook Lane."

"Good to know." He shuffled his feet a few times, kicking up dust. "It's been nice meeting you, Elma."

She gave a brief nod. "I enjoyed meeting you, too."

As they parted ways, Ben paused briefly and glanced over his shoulder. *Now I need to find some excuse to visit Elma's store.* Watching Elma walk away, he gave her a smile when she briefly looked back in his direction. Even from where he stood, Ben could see Elma's cheeks had turned pink.

When Ben approached his mother's table, he was surprised to see several people clustered around. Mom's face would scrunch up; then, breathing deeply, she'd release it, as though trying to regain her calm. He recognized that look as one of frustration.

Ben wasted no time in stepping behind the table and helping to wait on customers. From the looks of things, Mom had already sold most of her flowers, and the garden produce seemed to be going fast, too.

When the customers moved on, Mom turned to Ben with a frown. "Where have you been all this time? I thought you were only going to look around and wouldn't be gone long."

"Sorry, Mom. Guess the time got away from me." Ben explained the circumstances of how he'd met Elma Hochstetler and gone with her to have coffee and pie.

Mom's eyebrows squished together. "Hmm. . . That name sounds familiar. Did she say where she's from?"

He nodded. "She and her twin sister run a general store in Topeka, and. . ."

Mom snapped her fingers. "Now I remember. When I spent the day with my friend Eileen a few weeks ago, we visited a store run by a woman named Elma. I wonder if it could be the same person."

"I bet it is. I mean, how many stores could there be in Topeka run by a woman named Elma?" Ben scratched at a spot under his hat.

"Good point." Mom got out her handkerchief and wiped the perspiration from her forehead. "So how come you went off to have pie and coffee with her when you knew I was here at the table by myself?"

"Because I wanted pie and coffee, and since she was heading that way I figured I may as well tag along. It gave us a chance to get acquainted." Ben leaned against the table. "Besides, I didn't realize you had a bunch of customers. I wasn't even sure the market had officially opened." He glanced at his mother's flowers, toying with the idea of taking a potted plant over to Elma. He could say it was an apology for spilling her basket of produce.

Naw, I'd better not. He mentally shook his head. *Mom might ask me about it and give me a hard time.*

Ben's mother tipped her head from one side to the other, as though weighing the situation. "Are you sure that was all there was to it?"

"What do you mean?"

"Hearing the way you were talking about her, plus your wide-eyed expression at the mention of her name, makes me think you might be smitten with the young woman." Mom took a bag of raisins from her purse and ate a few.

"Why would you think that, Mom? I only met Elma today." *Am I really that transparent? Does Mom have any idea the strange feeling I had when I first looked in Elma's eyes?*

⟋⟍⟍

Dorothy sat for a time, but she needed to get up and take a walk. "Ben, would you mind watching our booth while I get some lemonade?"

"No problem, Mom. You go ahead and take a break."

"Do you need anything while I'm out?" She picked up her purse.

"I'm fine for now. The pie and coffee I had earlier is holding me." Ben rubbed his stomach and grinned.

"Okay, I'll be back soon." Dorothy started walking, looking further down the line of vendors. The place was full of people milling around. She knew right where the food places were located, so she headed in that direction. All she really had to do was follow her nose. Besides the drink Dorothy intended to buy for herself, she smelled kettle corn being made nearby, and it called to her. About the time she finished paying for a glass of lemonade, her friend Eileen tapped her shoulder.

Dorothy smiled. "Well, hello. I was hoping to see you here."

"I'm glad I made it today. As you can see, I've been shopping." Eileen held up a large paper bag. "How's it going at your booth so far?"

"I've sold a lot of my plants, and with Ben's help, we've kept up a nice pace."

"Good to hear. I've been slowly making my way around to your booth but hadn't made it that far yet." Eileen pointed across the way. "Why don't we take a seat over there at that table?"

"All right. It'll be nice to sit and chat." Dorothy stopped first to buy a bag of kettle corn; then they both found seats.

As they sat and talked, Dorothy told Eileen about Ben leaving their booth earlier to look around. "He was gone awhile, and it got real busy for me there by myself. I felt frustrated trying to juggle everything alone."

"You poor thing. I bet it was nerve wracking."

"Jah." Dorothy held the bag of kettle corn out to her friend. "Would you like some?"

"Danki." Eileen helped herself.

"Anyway, when Ben came back to our booth, he mentioned that he'd been off having pie and coffee with an Amish woman named Elma Hochstetler from Topeka."

Eileen's eyebrows rose. "Oh, jah, you and I were in her store a couple weeks ago. She's one of the owners of E&T's General Store."

Dorothy leaned closer, lowering her voice. "I think Ben might be smitten with this young lady."

"Really? What makes you believe so?"

"When he talked about her, he seemed to brighten up." Dorothy sipped on her drink. "Of course, he only met her today, so I probably shouldn't read much into it."

"I agree. A lot of young people today seem to be moving slower than we did at that age—not wanting to hurry into marriage and start a family."

Dorothy nodded. *I'm fine with that. Ben does need to find a wife, though. But not if she lives a good distance from Grabill. My world would be so different if he were to move far from home. I don't think I could deal with it.*

Chapter 12

Topeka

It had been two weeks since Elma went to the farmers' market in Shipshewana. She'd done fairly well with sales, but it wasn't likely she'd be able to rent another table there this month because things were busier than ever at the store. Elma couldn't help wondering if she might see Ben Wagler again if she went back to the market. He'd said he might drop by the store sometime, but he could have been making small talk or trying to be polite. More than likely, she'd probably never see him again. In the brief time they'd spent together, though, Elma found herself desiring to know Ben better. He had the kindest-looking eyes, and although his voice was deep, his tone was gentle. She could still visualize his warm smile.

Now don't start fantasizing about something that's not likely to happen, she scolded herself.

Elma glanced across the room to where Thelma sat behind the counter. Thelma looked more tired than usual today but was determined to be here for a few hours.

Lizzie was in the back, straightening some bolts of material, and then she was supposed to put out a box of thread that had just come in. Elma wasn't sure how much her helper had gotten done so far, because the last time she checked, Lizzie had been visiting with some of the customers. It wasn't a bad thing to chat with those who came into the store, but if given the chance, Lizzie could go on for hours.

With a shrug, Elma headed for the back room to check the list of supplies she needed to order. When she stepped inside, she took a seat at the desk and picked up her ordering tablet. She'd only been sitting a moment when she caught a movement out of the corner of her eye. It didn't take long for her to realize it was a little gray mouse.

Oh, great. Just what the store needs. I don't want the creepy rodent in here with me. Mice are disgusting creatures. If Tiger was in here right now, he'd go after the mouse.

Sliding her chair away from the desk, she picked up the broom in the corner of the room. "I don't need this," Elma muttered. Of course, the mouse was too quick for her and darted into a wee hole on the opposite side of the room. As much as Elma disliked the idea, she'd have to bring Tiger into the store.

⸺

Delbert pulled his horse up to the hitching rail outside Joseph's harness shop and stepped down from the buggy. He'd been in the area doing carpentry work for an Amish couple, so it was a good chance to drop by and say hello to his friend.

After making sure his horse was secure, Delbert opened the door to the harness shop. When he stepped inside, he was greeted by the smells of leather, savory neat's-foot oil, and pungent dye. Piled on the cement floor were bits of leather scraps resembling spaghetti noodles. An oversized sewing machine run by an air compressor sat on a large table, and a row of tools spilled out of round wooden holders on the workbench nearby.

Delbert moved past several harnesses and bridles looped from ceiling hooks and nearly ran into an enormous sheet of loosely rolled leather. "Where are ya, Joe?" he called.

A few seconds later, his longtime friend stepped out of the back room, grinning as he ambled toward him. "Well, well, I didn't expect to see you today." Joe grinned and slapped Delbert on the back.

Delbert explained his reason for being in town then asked how things were going.

"Ya mean here or at home?"

"Either or." Delbert leaned against the sewing machine table.

"Things at home are okay, although my fraa tends to do too much." Joseph folded his arms and groaned. "Here, things have been kinda slow the last few weeks, and it's got me worried."

Delbert shook his head. "No need for that. As long as there are Amish folks living in Topeka and the surrounding area, there will be a need for your harness shop."

"You're right about there being a need for a harness shop, but what if people who used to come in here decide to take their work someplace else?"

"That's not gonna happen. You have a reputation for doing good work. Things will pick up again soon, I'm sure."

"And if they don't?" Joseph dropped his gaze to the messy floor while rubbing his neck.

"I'm sure they will, but if for some reason they don't, then you'll look for something else to do."

Joseph's bottom lip pulled in. "I don't know how to do anything but make and repair harnesses, Dell."

Tired of standing, Delbert pulled a folding chair out from the wall and took a seat. "Are you still worried about whether you can support your family?"

Joseph looked up and nodded. "It won't be just me and Thelma anymore. In a few months, I'll be a daed, and there will be another mouth to feed."

Delbert snickered. "The boppli won't be eating solid food for some time after it's born, so you don't have to worry about that for a while."

"Very funny. You know what I mean."

"The best thing you can do is pray about the situation and let God take care of the rest."

"You're right. I made that decision once already, but I keep taking it back."

"Well, quit it." Delbert stood and draped his arm across his friend's shoulders. "Just remember, I'm here for you if you need to talk. Oh, and don't worry, 'cause I'd never stand by and let my best friend and his family starve." He noticed for the first time dark circles beneath his friend's eyes.

Joseph smiled. "Danki, Dell. You really are a good *freind*."

"Hey, let me take you out to lunch. I'll even drive, since I'm ready to go." Delbert fiddled with a piece of leather lying on the counter.

"Okay. Let me close things up and hang my RETURN AFTER LUNCH sign in the window. I can sure use a break. Maybe it'll help pick up my spirits." Joseph adjusted the sign on the door.

As they headed for town, Delbert asked which restaurant Joe would like to go to for lunch. He wasn't surprised when his friend chose his favorite place—Tiffany's.

Delbert snapped the reins to get his horse to pick up the pace. "You know, if you're worried about your business and wondering if you'll be able to support a family, I could teach you how to do carpentry work."

Joseph smirked, pulling off his straw hat. "I'm not sure I could learn that type of trade easily. Besides, I like what I do."

"It was only a suggestion."

"I appreciate it, and you'll be the first person I call upon if it comes to changing careers." Joseph swatted him with the hat before placing it back on his head.

Delbert pulled his rig into the restaurant parking lot. *Sure hope my pal's worries are for nothing. I hope and pray he can keep providing for his growing family.*

⌒

Grabill

"Sure appreciate you takin' me to LaGrange on such short notice," Ben told his driver, Dave Carlson, as they headed down the road in Dave's truck.

Dave tapped the steering wheel. "It's a good thing you caught me when you did, because I was heading out to do some fishing when the telephone rang."

Ben's jaw clenched. "Sorry about that. I would have called another driver if you'd said something."

Dave shook his bald head. "It's no big deal. I can always go fishing tomorrow." He glanced in his rearview mirror. "You sure your dog's gonna be okay back there?"

Ben turned his head to check, and he smiled at how the breeze from the moving truck made his dog's ears flap around. Nose sniffing the air, Hunter was obviously enjoying himself, watching the scenery whiz by. "Hunter's ridden in the bed of a truck before, so I'm sure he'll be fine."

Dave snickered. "I could see by the way he was carryin' on back at your place that he wanted to go along."

"Yeah, the dog thinks he should go everywhere with me, but most times, like when I'm going off to shoe a horse, he has to stay home with Mom." Ben reached into his pocket and pulled out a pack of gum. "I would have left Hunter home today, but with Mom not feeling well, I figured he'd bark and get on her nerves if I locked him in the kennel."

"You're probably right. He'd have most likely carried on the whole time you were gone."

Ben gave a nod before glancing at the cardboard box filled with flowers on the seat between them. A lady who bought some of Mom's flowers at the farmers' market two weeks ago had called and asked if she could get some more. Since Mom had come down with a bad cold and didn't feel like going out or exposing anyone, Ben had volunteered to take them. Afterward, if Dave didn't mind the detour, he planned to go to Topeka and stop by E&T's General Store to say hello. Elma had been on Ben's mind a lot since their meeting in Shipshewana. He was eager to get to know her better. At the very least, he needed to find out if she had a suitor.

∽

LaGrange

Ben was glad when he delivered the flowers to Velma Williamson, and she seemed pleased. "I was hoping your mother would have a table at the farmers' market again, but I guess she's been busy with other things." The elderly woman smiled when she gave Ben the money; then she tipped her head to one side. "Did you hear that sound?"

"What sound?"

"It came from outside, I think." She fiddled with her hearing aid. "I need a new battery for this thing. When the battery is low it buzzes sometimes."

"I didn't hear anything."

She waved a hand in the air. "Not important. Please tell your mother I hope she feels better soon, and I might be calling again for another order."

"Yes, I will." Ben couldn't imagine why Velma would need to buy more flowers when she had some growing in her own garden. With what he'd witnessed already, she appeared to be a bit eccentric. But if she wanted to spend her money that way, who was he to question it?

Ben said good-bye to Mrs. Williamson and hopped back in Dave's truck. He was about to ask if Dave would mind going to Topeka when he glanced back and noticed Hunter was no longer in the bed of the truck. He looked over at Dave. "What happened to my dog?"

Dave lifted both hands. "He jumped out when you headed up to the house with the flowers. Then I saw him running around the yard for a bit, chasing a black-and-white cat. Figured he'd be back in the truck by now."

"Well, he's not." Ben opened his door and jumped out. Scanning the yard, he cupped his hands around his mouth. "Hunter! Hunter! Where are ya, boy?"

No sign of the dog. Not even a bark in response to his call. Surely Hunter couldn't have gone too far. But then if he was after Velma's cat, they both could have taken off down the road.

Ben called Hunter's name a few more times, but still no response. A few minutes later, a scruffy-looking black-and-white cat darted into the yard and leaped onto the front porch. Ben expected to see Hunter come bounding in on the cat's heels, but no such luck.

He called the dog's name a few more times then stepped onto the porch and knocked on Velma's door. As soon as it opened, the cat zipped inside.

Velma tipped her head back, looking up at him with a quizzical expression. "Did you forget something, Ben?"

"Yeah, my dog."

Her mouth opened slightly. "Did you say your hog?"

Taking into consideration that Velma was slightly hard of hearing, Ben repeated, a little louder, "My dog. He was in the back of my driver's truck when I brought the flowers up to you, and now he's gone." No point mentioning that Hunter had been chasing her cat.

"Well, I haven't seen your dog, but if you'll give me a description, I'll call and let you know if I see him anywhere."

Ben closed his eyes briefly and took a deep breath. Apparently, Velma thought he would go home without his dog. Well, that wasn't going to happen. If it took the rest of the morning and all afternoon, Ben would find Hunter.

Chapter 13

Grabill

T hanks for the ride." Ben reached into his pocket and handed Dave the money he owed. "And I'm sorry for keepin' you most of the day."

Dave waved away his concerns. "Aw, that's okay. I'm just sorry we couldn't find your dog."

"Yeah, me, too." Ben's neck bent forward as he sagged against the seat. "Maybe, if I'm lucky, Hunter will find his way home."

"Could be. I've heard of some dogs traveling many miles to get back to their master."

Ben nodded, although his chest felt heavy. As much as he hated to admit it, he might never see Hunter again. Ben and Dave had driven around LaGrange for several hours after leaving Velma's house, but there was no sign of his dog. In addition to the possibility of losing a good hunting dog, they'd used up so much time looking for Hunter that he hadn't made it to Topeka to see Elma. He'd have to plan a trip there some other time. One thing was certain, if Hunter should return, he wouldn't be going any distance with Ben—especially not in the bed of a pickup truck.

"Well, I'd better let you go." Ben opened the truck door and stepped out. "Thanks again, Dave, for all you did today."

"No problem. Tell your mother I said hello and that I hope she feels better soon."

"I will." As Ben watched Dave's truck pull out of the yard, his mouth twisted grimly. He dreaded telling Mom that Hunter was gone. These past few years she'd grown attached to the dog, and it went without saying that Ben had, too. Unfortunately, he had a sinking feeling Hunter wasn't coming back.

Ben walked slowly toward the house; then wishful thinking made him glance toward the pastures. How many times had he and Hunter walked those fields together? Would it only be a memory now? Ben watched, almost willing Hunter to materialize and run toward him, hungry and eager to be fed his supper.

"Where are you, my furry friend?" Ben whispered, with one last look before going in. "I hope wherever you are tonight, someone will be kind to you."

$\sim$

LaGrange

When Delbert arrived home, he pulled his rig around back near the buggy shed and barn. The summery heat of the day made him happy to pull into some cool shade near the building. He climbed down, took off his hat, and fanned himself, leaning against his rig to rest a moment. His horse, Chip, stood snorting loudly and nodding his head.

"Okay, boy. I'll see to you in a moment." Delbert noticed his shirt was sweaty under his suspenders. He couldn't wait to eat, change, and relax when all the chores were done.

After unhitching Chip, he led him to the barn for a good brushing and offered fresh water to drink.

Today had been long, and Delbert looked forward to spending a quiet evening with his feet propped up. Since he didn't feel like heating up the kitchen by using the gas stove, he'd settle for a tuna sandwich and a few pickles with chips. He'd stopped at the grocery store on the way back from Topeka and bought a gallon of root beer, so he would have a tall glass of that, too. Good thing Elma wouldn't be there to watch him drink it. She'd probably have something to say about the high sugar count.

Delbert led the horse to the barn, and when he opened the stall door, the hinges squeaked. He'd need to get those oiled soon. Once the horse was inside, he grabbed the brush and currycomb. While Chip drank water and munched on some oats, Delbert wiped the animal down then began the combing and currying process.

The odor of straw tickled Delbert's nose. *Achoo! Achoo! Achoo!* He set the brush aside and pulled a hankie out of his pocket. Hay was one of the many things he was allergic to—especially as he'd gotten older. His sensitivities had worsened over the years, and he'd become intolerant to even more things than when he was young.

Sweat trickled down his face as he fought against the tangles in Chip's mane, but he persevered, despite his horse's snorting protests and hooves thumping against the wooden floor.

When the chore was done, Delbert put the comb and brush away, stepped out of the stall, and latched the door. His stomach rumbled, reminding him it was suppertime, so he would wait to put the buggy in the shed till after he'd had a bite to eat. A tuna sandwich sounded pretty good about now.

Stepping out of the barn and into the yard, Delbert paused to breathe in the fresh air. After being cooped up in the stuffy building, it felt good to be outside again.

When Delbert rounded the corner of his house, he came to a halt. "What's this?"

A German shorthair pointer, with liver-and-white spots on his head and back, lay on the porch, tongue hanging out. Delbert had never seen the hunting dog before and didn't have an inkling who the animal belonged to. Well, the critter couldn't stay here, but Delbert wouldn't let it languish in the hot sun, either, even though it would be setting before long.

As soon as Delbert stepped onto the porch, the dog whimpered and looked up at him with sorrowful brown eyes.

"I know, buddy. You look hot and tired. I'll get ya some water real quick." Delbert opened the door and stepped into the house, hoping the dog wouldn't follow. The last thing he needed was dirty paw prints or dog hair floating through the rooms. He glanced back, impressed to see the dog patiently waiting.

After filling a large plastic bowl with cool water, he went back outside. Placing the dish in front of the dog, Delbert stepped aside and watched. He had to admit, the animal was beautiful and seemed well behaved. As nice looking as this one was, there must be an owner searching for it.

With no hesitation, the critter began lapping the water until it was gone. Licking his lips and wagging his short, stubby tail, the dog sat, looking at Delbert as if he needed more.

"Okay, okay." Delbert picked up the bowl, went back in the house, and filled it again. This time the dog drank half the water then flopped onto the porch with a grunt and a burp.

"My, my, that must have been good." Delbert chuckled and patted his own stomach. "I know how you feel when your belly is satisfied."

Delbert took a seat and watched the animal rest. The dog appeared friendly enough. He noticed that the shorthair wore a collar, but after inspecting it, he saw no identification. Delbert figured now that the animal had been refreshed he'd move on, but the critter put his nose between his paws and slept.

Delbert didn't want to bother the dog, and the tuna sandwich he envisioned himself eating made his mouth water. He brought his hand up to his shoulder and massaged a knot that had developed.

I can't keep this hund. Delbert rolled his neck from side to side while giving an impatient huff. He wasn't allergic to all dogs. In fact, when he was a boy, he'd had the best dog ever. *But I'll never put myself through that again. Besides, this animal is not my problem. He can stay on the porch for now. But if he's not gone by morning, I'll ask around. I'm sure someone must know who owns the mutt.*

∽

Topeka

Elma glanced at the clock, relieved to see it was almost time to close the store for the day. No doubt there'd be something Lizzie had forgotten to do, which wasn't out of the ordinary on any given day. She could tell Lizzie's back was acting up again by the way she bent or reached in an odd position to do even the simplest of tasks.

Thelma had gone home a few hours ago, and Lizzie was in the back room gathering her things. An English woman and her son were still in the store, but Elma didn't want to rush the lady if she had more shopping to do. It wouldn't hurt to keep the store open a few minutes past closing time.

Elma went over by the garden clogs, looking at what was left from the inventory. She'd run a half-off special on the older styles so she'd have ample floor space for the newer versions. It appeared there were only two pairs left, so Elma would need to bring out the new ones with fun colors.

As mother and son approached the candy aisle, Elma overheard the young boy ask if he could have a candy bar.

"No, son," his mother responded. "You had candy earlier today, and too much sugar isn't good for you."

The boy pouted, but the mother held firm.

Elma smiled then headed to the counter to tidy up the work-space. It was nice to know she wasn't the only person who objected to sugar-laden treats. Silently, she commended the woman for not giving in to her son. She'd witnessed too many mothers who came to the store give in to a whiny child's wishes in order to keep the child quiet or from throwing a temper tantrum.

Elma pursed her lips. *If I ever become a mother, I hope I'll be able to practice tough love.* While it would be difficult not to give in to children's wants, it wouldn't be good for them to have their way all the time. Up at the front, Elma took a seat on the stool. She slid the notepad over and wrote a reminder to herself to check for healthier snacks to sell in the store. *I believe we need a good array of both types. I'd like to offer my customers something for on the go that is better for their health.*

A short time later, the English woman, wearing an ample amount of perfume, placed her purchases on the counter.

Elma held her breath. *I'll have to open up the front door and air the place out after this woman leaves.* Her nose twitched, and she glanced toward the front entrance.

As Elma rang up the items, the child darted back up the candy aisle. She was tempted to follow, but that was up to his mom. No doubt he hoped to convince his mother that he should have the candy bar he'd asked for previously.

The boy's mother, dressed in a bright green printed dress, glanced over her shoulder, then back to Elma. "When he gets something going in his mind, it's hard to reason with him. Do you have any children?"

"No." Elma reached for the next item, examining it to find the price.

"My name is Corine, and we're new to the area. Well, I'm actually not new. I lived here for a few years when I was a kid. Anyway, we're still trying to settle down from the hectic move." She cupped her hands around her mouth and turned around. "Ronnie, hurry up now!" She stuffed a hand, weighted with bold jewelry, into her large handbag and fumbled through to retrieve her billfold.

"Where are you from?" Elma questioned.

"Pennsylvania. I was married for a time, but now it's just me and my son. We came back to my old stomping grounds. Ronnie will have his grandparents and me to watch him grow." Corine smiled, showing the whitest teeth.

Once Corine's purchases were paid for and Elma had bagged everything up, the woman looked at her and said, "Thank you. I hope you have a nice evening."

Elma smiled. "And you as well."

"Come on, Ronnie, it's time to go," Corine called as she started for the front door.

A few second later, the towheaded boy ran up to his mother and followed her out the door.

Lizzie came out of the back room then and asked if Elma needed her for anything else.

"No, and I'm ready to close up for the day." Elma gave Lizzie's arm a tender squeeze. "See you tomorrow morning."

"You can count on it." Lizzie lifted her chin and sniffed the air. "Wow, that's some mighty strong toilet water someone splashed on today."

Elma rolled her eyes. "I agree. Lizzie, would you please do me a favor and prop the door open on your way out? I don't need the strong perfume odor clinging to everything in the room."

"No problem."

As soon as her helper went out the door, Elma moved from the counter and stepped up to the window, watching Lizzie disappear around the corner. She flipped over the CLOSED sign and turned off the battery-operated fans, shut off most of the gas lamps, and made sure Tiger wasn't in the store. She'd been letting him inside every morning, and it seemed to help keep the mice population down. However, she didn't want the cat to remain in the store overnight. Elma needed him in the house with her, if for nothing else but companionship.

While Elma aired out the store, she walked down the toy aisle to turn off the overhead lamp. There, she discovered a crumpled-up candy wrapper behind a wooden truck. She frowned. *I'll bet that little English boy took a candy bar and ate it, despite what his mother said. If they return to the store, I'll have to keep a closer watch on the little* schtinker.

Chapter 14

LaGrange

When Delbert got up Saturday morning, he made a decision. The dog, after three days, was still on the front porch, always looking up at him as if to say, "Please take me in."

"Guess that's what I get for feeding the mutt and letting him sleep on the porch." Delbert grimaced. Despite having asked around the area, no one knew who owned the German shorthair.

"Sorry, buddy, but I'm not a bird hunter, so I don't need a hunting dog." Delbert pulled out his hankie and blew his nose, trying not to think of the past. "In addition to that, I'm allergic to cats as well as some dogs. Maybe I'm not sensitive to you, but the last thing I need is a pet."

Delbert had vowed many years ago that he'd never own another dog. The pain he went through when he was a boy stuck with him even after all these years. How other people could go right out and get another pet after losing the one they loved was beyond him. Delbert realized it was normal for a person to outlive a pet, but he was not one of those people willing to go through such anguish again. That solemn day, as his dog of nine years lay lifeless in his arms, Delbert's heart felt as if it were torn in two. Even his dad said Sadie was the best rabbit dog he'd ever seen, but unfortunately, her zealousness was what got her killed. Delbert could still see Sadie chasing a bunny around the yard, and when it ran across the road, the dog followed. After that, it was like watching in slow motion as Sadie's life was snuffed out by an oncoming car. It was an image that to this day, Delbert would never forget.

Woof! Woof! The German shorthair wagged his tail and pawed at

Delbert's pant leg, pulling his thoughts aside.

Looking upward, he groaned. "Why me?"

Unable to resist, Delbert went down on his knees to pet the friendly animal. Its hair was short, and after scratching behind the pointer's ears for a while, Delbert was surprised he hadn't started sneezing. In fact, his nose didn't even tickle anymore.

Already this dog was worming his way into Delbert's heart as he shared a dish of leftovers from his ham and egg breakfast. "Well, it's not going to happen again." Delbert shook his head. "Since I don't know who your owner is, and I'm not gonna keep ya, it's time for me to find you a new home."

⌒

Grabill

Ben sat at the breakfast table with his head in his hands.

Dorothy tapped his shoulder. "Are you missing your hund?"

He lifted his head and gave a slow nod.

"I miss Hunter, too. He was a good watchdog and kept me company when you were at work."

"Jah." Ben reached for his cup of coffee and took a drink. "I was hoping by now he'd have the good sense to find his way home, but it doesn't look like that's gonna happen."

"Maybe you should go back to LaGrange and look around some more." Dorothy handed Ben a plate of blueberry muffins.

He shook his head. "No thanks, Mom, I've had enough to eat, and I should get busy and finish the rest of my chores that I didn't get done earlier this morning."

"What about Hunter? Are you going to go looking for him?"

"I don't think so. I mean, what would be the point? He got out of Dave's truck while we were in LaGrange, but he could be anywhere by now."

"You're right." Dorothy helped herself to another muffin, grateful that her cold was better and her taste buds had returned. During the worst of her illness, not much appealed, and what she had eaten had no taste at all. To make matters worse, Dorothy's nose had been so stuffed up she'd been unable to smell any tantalizing aromas. Now, as she ate the blueberry treat, slathered with creamy butter, Dorothy enjoyed every morsel.

"Wish I'd left him home with you. It's my fault the hund is missing." Ben pushed his chair away from the table with a noisy scrape across the floor. "I'm headin' outside now, Mom. As soon as I'm done with the chores I'll be working out in the fields."

"Okay, I'll see you at lunchtime, then."

Dorothy watched her son go out the door, head down and shoulders slumped. She closed her eyes and prayed for Ben—for his dog to come home, and also that he'd find the perfect helpmate soon, because every man deserved a good wife.

Opening her eyes, Dorothy remembered she hadn't planned anything yet to include Martha Graber for a meal. *I'll call her later today and see if she'd be free to join us for supper one night next week. Maybe having Martha over will lift my son's spirits and put his mind on matters of the heart.*

⌒

Topeka

"How'd things go at the store this afternoon?" Thelma asked as she and Elma sat on her front porch, drinking ice-cold lemonade.

Elma sighed. "Busy as usual. It was hard for me and Lizzie to keep up."

"You should have let me stay and help you."

Elma shook her head. "You needed to come home and rest. Besides, we managed okay."

"You always seem to manage, but not always so easily." Thelma shifted in her chair when the baby kicked. She placed both hands against her stomach. "This little one has been quite active all day."

Elma moved her chair closer to Thelma's. "Can I feel it?"

"Of course." Thelma placed Elma's hand on the spot where the baby had been moving. "Feel that?"

Elma's eyes lit up. "I sure do. It must be wunderbaar knowing you're gonna become a mudder in a few months."

"It truly is." Thelma placed her hand over Elma's and gave it a pat. "Your turn will come. You'll see."

Elma crossed her arms, leaning back in her chair. "As much as

I would like to be married, I'm not holding out hope. I am past my prime, Thelma, and the truth is, I may never find the right man."

Thelma tapped her fingernails on the arm of her chair. *Should I tell my sister about Delbert calling this morning to say he'd be coming by later in the day? Would Elma decline my offer to stay for supper if she knew I'd invited Delbert to join us?* Thelma didn't want her sister to think she was playing matchmaker, but it was only last month when she'd invited Delbert for a cookout without Elma knowing.

Thelma cleared her throat. "When Joe gets home, he's going to cook some chicken on the grill. You will stay and join us, I hope."

Elma smiled. "That'd be nice. I made some gluten-free, dark chocolate brownies that are also sugar-free before going to work this morning. I'm enjoying the recipes from the all-natural cookbook I picked up in town." Her voice grew louder. "I've even gone through the book and dog-eared several of the pages. I can bring the brownies over, and we'll have them for dessert."

Thelma licked her lips. "That sounds good, and before I forget, how is Pearl's leg? It's been a little over a month now since she cut it on the nail. Just wondered how much longer until you can start using her again."

"Well, she is still under the vet's care, but the antibiotics and salve must be working because he says she's healing pretty well. The nail seems to be staying in place, too, after I hammered it back in. I sure don't want it to happen again." Elma paused. "I felt bad I didn't see that nail before."

"But everything is okay now, and that's what matters." Thelma licked her lips again. "Now, about those brownies. . . I have vanilla ice cream we can serve with them."

"Think I'll run over to my house and get them right now." Elma stood, smoothing the wrinkles in her long blue dress.

"Okay. I'll go inside and set things out to make a tossed green salad. Joseph should be here soon, and we'll eat after he grills the meat."

༄

Elma smiled as she put the brownies in a plastic container. It would be nice to eat supper with family this evening. It had been a few weeks since they'd cooked out together, and this time Delbert wouldn't be there. Surely Thelma would have said something if she'd planned to invite him. *I need time to relax with my family. It'll be a lot better than sitting at the kitchen table by myself with Tiger staring up at me, meowing.*

Maybe I should get a dog to keep me company. Elma thought about Joseph's dog, Ginger, and how she seemed almost human sometimes. Of course a dog couldn't carry on a conversation, or help with one's chores. But at least it wouldn't disagree with her if she said something it didn't like, and the best part was, most dogs were eager to please.

"Well, I don't have a dog, and I'm not going out of my way to look for one, so I'd better be satisfied with Tiger for now." Elma picked up the brownie container and went out the door. She'd fed and watered the chickens earlier and also checked on Pearl, so the only thing she'd need to do when she got home later this evening was let Tiger in the house and give him some food and fresh water.

Walking through the grass, Elma stopped when she stepped on something hard. Bending down to see what it was, she moved the blades about with her hands. "Ach, my keys!" After all these weeks, Elma could hardly believe her missing keys had been found. Of course, they were useless now, since Delbert had already replaced the locks. At least she had the consolation of knowing no one else had found them.

Glancing both ways before crossing the street, Elma headed up the driveway leading to Thelma and Joseph's house. As she drew closer, she saw a horse and buggy at the hitching rail near the barn. At first, she thought it belonged to Joseph, but after approaching the gelding, she recognized it as Delbert's horse, Chip. *Oh, no! Not again. I wonder what he's doing here. Is Delbert staying for supper? If so, why didn't my sister tell me?* Even though Thelma hadn't admitted it, Elma suspected her twin was hoping she and Delbert would get back together.

When Elma rounded the corner of the house, she spotted Delbert standing near the picnic table with a beautiful spotted dog at his side. As she approached cautiously, the dog's ears perked up, and he left Delbert to rub against her leg. Elma reached out to let the dog smell her hand, and right away, he licked her fingers.

"He's a friendly one." Delbert joined Elma.

"What a beautiful hund." She bent down to pet the dog's silky head. "Is he yours, Delbert?"

"No, not really. When I got home Wednesday afternoon, the critter was lying on my porch, lookin' like he was half-dead. I haven't found his owner, and I was hoping maybe Joe might take him."

Joseph stepped up to them and pointed under the picnic table, where Ginger lay sleeping. "One hund is enough for me. Besides, if I had another, Ginger would probably be jealous."

The shorthair moved his head from side to side and slurped Elma's hand with his long, wet tongue.

Elma didn't know what she was thinking, but with one hand on the dog's head, she turned to Delbert and said, "I'll take the hund. I think he likes me."

He gave a nod. "I believe you're right."

Elma turned to Thelma when she joined them on the lawn. "Oh, guess what I found before coming over here?"

Thelma shrugged and turned both hands upward.

"Found my missing keys to the store and house."

"That's good." Thelma moved closer. "Too bad you didn't find them sooner, though."

"Hopefully you won't lose your new set of keys," Delbert put in.

Ignoring his comment, Elma lifted the container she held. "Here's the dessert I brought. Should I take it inside?"

"Jah. I'll go with you. I'm not quite done with the salad."

Elma followed her sister into the house. Nearing the open window, she tipped her head back and sniffed the air. "Smells like Joe has the meat grilling already. I can hardly wait to eat."

Thelma nodded. "I'm getting hungerich myself." She giggled, rubbing her stomach. "Or should I say *we* are getting hungry?"

Elma laughed. It was good to see her sister in a joyful mood. Being married to Joseph and now expecting her first baby—what more could she ask for to fulfill her life?

For a few seconds, Elma's jealousy took over. She and Thelma had always done everything together. It didn't seem right that Elma had no one.

CHAPTER 15

Grabill

When Ben came home from shoeing a horse the following Wednesday evening, he was exhausted and ready to relax. He only had a few things that needed to be done, and then he planned to put up his feet and unwind the rest of the evening.

Ben's tiredness didn't stop him from pausing to listen to the cicadas singing, however. "Sure can tell it's almost August." He reached up to rub a knot in his shoulder. Where had this year gone? Summer would soon be over.

While he listened to the insects' rhythmic chorus, he meandered toward the house. Surprised to see Martha holding a bouquet as she stood beside Mom near her flower garden, Ben halted. Assuming she must have come by to purchase the daisies, he said a quick hello and headed for the house.

"I invited Martha to join us for supper," Mom called as Ben stepped onto the porch.

Hoping to conceal his frustration, he halted and forced a smile before turning around. "I didn't realize we had company coming tonight. I was planning to muck out the barn after we eat, so I wasn't gonna take a shower till it was done."

"Can't it wait until tomorrow?" Mom's hands fluttered like she'd lost track of what she was doing. Ben recognized his mother's way of covering up her disappointment. He had a hunch she'd set this meal up so he could spend time with Martha.

"Never mind. It's no big deal." Ben waved a hand. "I'll clean out the barn after work tomorrow."

Feet shuffling as she kicked at the ground with her shoe, Martha mumbled, "Maybe I should go. I don't want to interrupt your plans."

Ben shook his head. "No, it's okay. I'll go take a shower and change clothes. Then I'll be ready for supper." He stepped into the house and closed the door. *Poor Martha. She keeps being dragged into my mother's plan to make us a couple. I doubt Martha has any more interest in me than I do her. Mom could use a new hobby to keep herself busy.* He reached up to rub his shoulder again. *Sure wish she would stop meddling. If it's meant for me to have a wife, I'd like to pick my own.*

⁓

Ben couldn't wait to eat. He'd worked up a good appetite and taken his spot at the head of the table. They bowed their heads for silent prayer, and when finished, Ben's mother passed the food to him. Ben took what he wanted and passed the plates to Martha in awkward silence, unsure of what to say. Mom appeared to be compensating for his lack of conversation, as she chatted away to their guest.

Meanwhile, Ben couldn't help wondering what Elma might be doing. He nudged the potatoes on the plate with his fork, allowing his attention to keep on its detour. *I wonder what she's having for supper tonight. Can't wait to get up to Topeka to see her again.*

"Did you have many horses to shoe today?"

Ben's head jerked at Martha's question. "Uh. . .jah, I did."

"Do you enjoy shoeing horses?"

He nodded.

Mom passed him the platter of meat. "Would you like some more beef, Ben?"

"Jah, sure." He forked two pieces then handed the platter to Martha. The distraction of eating and having one's mouth full of food made it easier not to talk.

"This roast beef is so delicious and tender." Martha smiled at Mom from across the table.

"Danki. I'm glad you like it." Mom glanced at Ben, sitting at the head of the table, silently poking at his mashed potatoes. "How's your new job at Country Sales going, Martha?" Mom asked.

"It's going well. I enjoy working there." Martha blotted her lips with a napkin. Looking over at Ben, she smiled.

Mom gestured to the platter of meat. "Would you like another piece of beef?"

He stabbed one with his fork and passed the plate to Martha without making eye contact with her.

When the meal was over, he excused himself and headed for the comfort of the recliner in the living room. After Ben took a seat, he adjusted the footrest and put up his feet. "Ah, this feels good. Now I can relax and allow Mom's good meal to digest."

Ben heard his mom and Martha chatting in the other room, but he couldn't make out their words. He figured they were busy clearing away the dishes and putting the leftovers in the refrigerator.

Martha was all right, but she didn't seem mature enough for him. She was nice looking, too, but in his judgment, Elma was prettier. Ben couldn't help comparing the young women.

Redirecting his thoughts, Ben remembered a customer he needed to call for a time adjustment, since he'd forgotten about his dental appointment next week. Trying to let his mind go blank, he closed his eyes. It took no time for his thoughts to return to Elma. *If she isn't being courted by anyone, I'd like to ask her to have supper with me.* Ben laced his fingers together and rested them under his head. His eyelids became heavy while he thought of the pretty young woman who lived in Topeka.

⌒

Dorothy closed her eyes briefly and took a deep breath. Had Ben still been a little boy, she would have scolded him. Martha was their guest, and he should have known better than to treat her that way. She wasn't about to give up, but she couldn't force Ben to talk to Martha, either. Maybe he'd be more cordial if the two of them were alone.

After Ben retired to the living room, Martha started clearing the table, beginning with the bowl of mashed potatoes.

"Oh, never mind about that." Dorothy came around the table and took the bowl from their guest. "There aren't many dishes, and I can manage fine on my own. Why don't you join Ben in the living room? It'll give you two a better chance to visit."

Martha drew her mouth into a straight line while biting down on her bottom lip. "Are—are you sure?"

"Absolutely." Dorothy gestured toward the archway leading to the other room, shooing her in that direction. "Go on now. I'll be fine."

Martha offered a quick smile and left the room. A few seconds later, she was back. "Umm. . .Ben is asleep in his chair." Before Dorothy could comment, the young woman said she would finish clearing the table.

Heaving a sigh, Dorothy ran warm water in the kitchen sink and added liquid detergent. "As soon as we finish the dishes I'll wake him up."

Martha shook her head. "Oh, no, please don't. He's obviously tired and needs his sleep. I guess he worked too hard today."

Or else he's not interested in a relationship with you. Dorothy gripped the sponge and picked up a plate. *Should I give up on this or keep trying to get Ben and Martha together?*

Topeka

Thelma sat beside Joseph on the couch, writing a letter to her parents. Even though she could easily make a phone call and leave a message asking to set up a time so they could talk, she liked keeping in touch through the mail. Thelma enjoyed making her own cards and stationery, too. She'd made some spring-themed cards a while back, with friends and family in mind, to replenish her supply. The card she'd chosen to send her parents was detailed with flowers, like some Mom grew in her yard.

Sitting here in shared silence as their day wound down gave Thelma an opportunity to jot down her thoughts and make sure she was giving Mom and Dad all the details of what was going on in her and Joseph's life, as well as Elma's.

While Thelma wrote the letter, her husband read the latest edition of *The Budget* newspaper. He'd been quiet this evening, and Thelma wondered if something might be bothering him. A couple of times, she heard him sigh. If it was anything major, she was sure Joseph would talk about it in his own good time.

Thelma felt a flutter in her stomach, followed by a powerful kick. The baby was quite active these days. It was a good thing, though. It meant everything with her pregnancy was going as it should.

She set her card aside and clasped Joseph's arm. "I think our boppli is playing a game of shuffleboard tonight."

Squinting, he set the paper on his lap. "What do you mean?"

"He or she kicks on one side and then the other." Thelma took hold of his hand, placing it against her belly—first on the right side, then on the left. "See what I mean?"

Joseph's eyes widened, and his mouth opened slightly. "You're right. Doesn't that bother you? I mean, is it painful?"

She laughed. "No, it's not painful, and it doesn't bother me much when I'm up and about. Sometimes, though, when I'm in bed trying to sleep, all that movement can keep me awake."

He clasped her hand. "That's why it's important for you to rest during the day—to make up for lost sleep at night."

"I know. My sister reminds me to take it easy all the time."

"Speaking of Elma, how's she gettin' along with the hund Dell gave her?"

"Okay, I guess." Thelma shrugged. "I sure never expected she would want a dog—especially when she brings the katz in the house at night."

c⁀

Tucking her feet under a throw pillow, Elma curled up on the couch, exhausted after another busy day at the store. Tonight, however, she didn't feel as lonely as before. Along with Tiger, she now had the companionship of a dog, and he seemed to like her as much as she did him. In fact, the German shorthair lay curled on the throw rug in front of the couch. Every once in a while, he would lift his head, look up at Elma, and whimper. In response to his bid for attention, she reached out and stroked the dog's head.

Tiger, on the other hand, wasn't fond of the new stranger and avoided the dog. The striped cat took fresh pathways lending him cover behind or under the furniture. In most cases, if the dog saw the cat, he'd do his bird dog stance before the chasing started. Much to

Elma's chagrin, Tiger would leap for the countertops in the kitchen or other high places, making loud hissing noises in disapproval.

Since Elma didn't know the dog's name, she decided to call him Freckles because of all the liver-and-white spots on his body. He was a well-behaved animal and responded eagerly to most anything she told him to do. Elma hadn't been sure how things would go the first night she'd brought Freckles into her house. It hadn't taken him long to spot Tiger and start a merry chase around the house. But when Elma clapped her hands and hollered, "Stop! Leave the poor cat alone!" Freckles dropped to the floor and put his nose between his paws. From that moment on, all Elma had to do when she wanted the dog to obey was clap her hands and say, "Stop!" Apparently his previous owner had done a good job teaching him to mind.

Elma's foot tingled when it began to fall asleep, and Freckles didn't even lift his head as she sat up to stretch her leg. After a few twirls of her ankle, the circulation returned.

She looked down at the dog and smiled when he shifted his position, never opening his eyes. "Crazy mutt." Two years ago, she'd have had a conniption if a dog or cat had come into her house, and she certainly would never have invited them in. But she'd become used to Tiger being in the house, and now here was another animal invading her domain.

I'm surprised Delbert didn't want to keep the hund, especially since Joseph has Ginger. Elma remembered how when they'd all gone fishing and Joseph brought Ginger along, Delbert seemed to like the dog. Maybe because of his work, he didn't want to be tied down with a pet. Elma had to admit she was glad he'd given the German shorthair to her.

Freckles lay contentedly as she ran her bare foot down the middle of his back, enjoying the feel of the animal's smooth, shiny coat. He thumped his tail on the floor and gave a contented grunt before going back to sleep.

I wonder where Freckles came from and who his master is. Elma yawned and lay back down, closing her eyes. *Could the person who used to own this beautiful animal be missing him tonight?*

Chapter 16

"I can hardly believe it's the first Monday of August already," Lizzie announced when she entered the store.

"I know," Elma agreed. "Seems like just the other day we turned over the calendar to the month of July. Now, here we are beginning a brand-new month." She pointed to the stand-up perpetual calendar on one end of the counter.

"Sometimes I wish I could slow the hands of time." Pursing her lips, Lizzie gave a slight shake of her head. "Then there are other times when I'm waiting for something and I wish I could speed things up." She moved closer to Elma.

"I understand." Elma left the stool where she'd been sitting. "Lizzie, why don't you sit here and take care of customers as they check out? When it's time for lunch we'll trade off."

Lizzie's eyes shone as she nodded her head. "It's fine with me."

Elma figured her helper would probably do a lot of visiting when people brought their purchases to her, but what other choice did she have? Thelma had a doctor's appointment this morning and wouldn't be available to work in the store until tomorrow, and then only for half a day. Elma had almost gotten used to Lizzie's continual chatter and sometimes eccentric ways. The customers didn't seem to mind, as they chatted with Lizzie about various things.

Elma smiled. There was no doubt about it—the elderly woman kept things interesting here in the store. There was never a dull moment with Lizzie around.

"Oh, before I forget. . ." Lizzie put her canvas tote on the counter.

"My friend Miriam, from Kendallville, came to visit me on Saturday and brought a bag of peaches. There's a farm near her where you can pick your own."

"Fresh peaches. They are so good this time of year." Elma's mouth watered, thinking about their sweet, juicy taste. "I can't remember the last time I had a good peach."

"Well, think no more." Lizzie opened the bag. "I sure can't eat all of them, so I brought you some. You can share with Thelma and her husband, too."

Elma watched while Lizzie laid all the peaches out on the counter. "They're beautiful." She picked one up. "I may have to wash this off right now and eat it."

Then Elma's eyes widened as Lizzie put a plastic container on the counter.

"I also made a peach pie." Lizzie beamed when she held up the pie dish. "Thought we could have some for dessert after our lunch today."

"Goodness, now I hope the morning goes fast. I'm already looking forward to lunch." Elma gave Lizzie a hug. "Danki for being so thoughtful."

"Think nothing of it. It's my pleasure." Lizzie waved her hand. "If I had kinner, I'd be baking for them all the time. Except for my brother, you and your sister are the closest thing I have to family."

"Thelma and I think a lot of you, too." Elma felt fortunate to have this wonderful lady helping in the store. Not because Lizzie gave her peaches and a pie, but because Elma had begun to see Lizzie as more than an employee. She hadn't thought about it much before, but this dear woman spent extra time with customers because she was lonely and enjoyed being with people. Not that she hadn't liked Lizzie before, but from here on out, Elma would consider this caring woman a friend.

Elma couldn't imagine not having her family nearby. It was bad enough her parents lived several hours away; thank goodness Thelma was close.

"I'm going in the back to straighten a few things and unload the rest of the material that was delivered last week." Elma gathered up the peaches and pie to put with their lunches in the back. "At lunchtime, we can divvy up some of the peaches for Thelma and Joe."

Lizzie nodded. "I'll be right here if you need me."

Elma started walking, but Lizzie called out to her again. "I forgot to ask. How's that new hund of yours doing?"

Elma turned to face her. "Freckles is getting along fine. I'm keeping him in the basement when I'm here at the store, until I can hire someone to build a kennel for him. I'm not about to let the dog have free run of the house when I'm not there." Elma shook her head. "There'd be too many temptations."

"Maybe your brother-in-law could do it." Lizzie rested her dimpled hands in her lap.

"He'd probably be willing, but I may ask Delbert, since he has carpentry skills."

"You've had him do a lot of things for you, jah?" Lizzie peered over the top of her glasses with a curious expression.

Elma nodded. "Both here and in my home."

"Is there something going on between you two?" Lizzie leaned forward, rubbing her hands together.

A rush of heat covered Elma's cheeks. "Now don't get any ideas about me and Delbert. We're just friends."

Lizzie's brows jiggled up and down. "Doesn't love begin with friendship?"

"Ach, Lizzie! Now who said anything about love?"

The older woman chuckled, putting her hand over her heart. "Guess I'm an old romantic." Her brows gathered in, and she looked downward. "Although I'll never really known what it's like to fall in love."

"Now don't you fret, Lizzie. Thelma and I love you, and your family does, too." It was all Elma could think to say. After all, she was in the same boat and had never known what true romantic love felt like.

Lizzie reached for a tissue and blew her nose. "Well, I mustn't keep you from what you'd planned to do. Besides, I heard a vehicle pulling in, which means we have a prospective customer."

"Right, and I'll let you take care of that while I do my thing."

"Okie-dokie."

⤳

"If you don't mind waiting for me, I shouldn't be too long," Ben told his driver when he pulled his truck up to E&T's General Store.

"No problem. Take your time." Dave picked up a paperback book. "I'll get a bit of reading done."

Ben opened the door and hopped out of the truck. After all these weeks of waiting, he looked forward to seeing Elma again. Now that he was within a short distance of her, his palms grew sweaty.

When he entered the store, he saw an older woman sitting behind the counter on a wooden stool. It certainly wasn't Elma or her twin. This had to be the right store, but maybe Elma and her sister weren't working today.

"Excuse me." Ben stepped up to the counter. "Is Elma Hochstetler here?"

The Amish woman stared at him, her eyelids blinking rapidly behind her metal-framed glasses. "Yes, she is. Would you like me to get her?"

He gave a quick nod. "If you don't mind."

"Since I have no other customers at the moment, I don't mind a'tall." She stepped off the stool and ambled toward the back of the store.

Ben rubbed a damp hand down his pant leg, taking a couple of quick breaths. He hoped he wasn't being too forward coming here. But ever since he'd met Elma at the farmers' market he had looked forward to seeing her again. Thoughts of her had come to mind each day since he'd met her. Now, as he stood leaning against the counter, he had a sudden desire to flee. What if she wasn't happy to see him? What if she thought he was being too forward coming here?

Maybe I could make some sort of excuse—say I came to buy something. Ben's muscles twitched as he took another calming breath and glanced around the store. What could be taking so long? Didn't the Amish woman know where Elma was?

Two women entered the store—one Amish, one English. They glanced at him briefly; then each headed down a different aisle.

Ben felt a trickle of sweat roll down his nose. He pulled a hankie from his pocket and wiped it away. A few seconds later, the older woman returned, but no Elma.

Ben cleared his throat. "Did you tell Elma I came to see her?"

"I did, but when she asked who you were, I said I didn't know 'cause I forgot to ask."

"I'm Ben Wagler. Elma and I met at the farmers' market a few weeks ago."

Grinning, the older woman sized him up and down then turned and ambled off once more. Ben's irrational fears began to take over again. He flexed his fingers, curling and uncurling them into the palms of his hands. Then he began cracking each knuckle. He'd come all this way and wasn't going to leave until he saw Elma.

Sure hope this green shirt I'm wearing isn't too wrinkled. Ben glanced at the bedraggled straw hat in his hands. *What was I thinking wearing this old thing today?*

While continuing to wait, he stood with his back against the counter. Looking around, he noticed how clean the place looked, although the building had an old smell to it. Everything looked quite organized, too. He liked that, since he kept all his tools in place on his workbench in the barn.

He watched the English woman who'd come into the store browsing near the back with her head lowered, while her Amish friend flitted about, holding on to her list and a basket for her purchases.

Leaning back farther, Ben tried to relax. *I wish the older woman who'd been sitting up here earlier would hurry back with Elma. What could be taking so long?*

A few more minutes went by; then there was Elma—smiling sweetly and extending her hand. "It's nice to see you again, Ben. What brings you into our store today?"

Ben felt relieved, seeing her positive response to his visit. He moistened his lips while clearing his throat. "I. . .uh. . .said I might come by sometime." Ben's nerves were heightened merely looking at her.

"Yes, you did. I just wasn't sure—"

"Came to see if you'd like to go out to lunch with me." Surprised by his own boldness, Ben touched his throat. "That is, if you're not too busy."

"I'd like to, Ben, but I can't today." Elma's shoulders drooped slightly. "My helper, Lizzie, and I are the only ones working at the store right now, and I can't leave her alone in case we get busy." Elma glanced down one of the aisles toward where Lizzie was helping some customers.

"Oh, I see." Ben couldn't hide his disappointment. "Maybe another time, then."

"That would be nice." Elma grabbed a notebook and pen and jotted down her phone number. Smiling, with a sincere expression, she lowered her voice. "The next time, though, please call ahead when you know you'll be in the area again, and I'll make sure my sister and Lizzie are both working here that day so I'm free to have lunch with you."

Ben smiled, speaking softer as well. "Okay, I'll do that." Well, at least she hadn't said she didn't want to be with him. He glanced around. "Since I'm here, maybe I'll do a little shopping."

She smiled. "Is there anything in particular you're looking for? Anything I can help you find?"

Ben shuffled his feet, looking anxiously about. "Well, maybe a new straw hat, if you have those here."

"We certainly do. If you'll come with me, I'll show you where they're located."

I would follow you anywhere, Elma. Ben clamped his teeth together, afraid he might blurt out the words.

Elma led the way, and Ben followed, his mouth getting drier by the minute. *Sure hope I don't say anything stupid.* He swallowed, wishing he had a bottle of water with him.

As they approached the shelf where men's hats were sold near the front of the store, Ben heard the roar of an engine outside. As the sound grew closer, he glanced out the window and watched in horror as a car approached, barreling toward the store. Before Ben could react or say anything, there was a crash, and the floor shuddered as if there'd been an earthquake. The hats vibrated off the shelf, and with a high-pitched squeal, Elma fell back into Ben's outstretched arms.

CHAPTER 17

A re you all right?" Ben clasped Elma's trembling shoulders, turning her to face him.

"I—I think so." Elma wasn't sure if her limbs felt weak from the shock of the crashing sound or the nearness of Ben as he held on to her arms. "Wh–what just happened?" Her voice quivered as she stepped to one side.

"I don't know, but we'd better go see."

As Elma and Ben moved toward the front door, Lizzie joined them, her face turning ashen. "I've never heard such a commotion. What on earth happened?"

"I believe a vehicle hit the store." Ben opened the front door. "Sure hope no one was seriously injured. Let me make sure the porch and steps are still sound."

Stepping out the door, Ben bounced his weight as he checked out the structural integrity of the porch and steps. "Nothing looks damaged here, at least, but I see where the vehicle has ended up." Ben waved the ladies over, and when Elma and Lizzie looked down, they gasped. The front bumper of a car, with its motor still running, was pushed up against one side of the store's basement wall. An elderly English woman sat inside, gripping the sides of her head.

Before Elma could react, Ben leaped off the porch, jerked the car door open, and turned off the ignition. At the same time, a man sitting in a pickup truck, who Elma assumed was Ben's driver, rushed to the scene.

Elma hurried down the stairs, joining Ben by the side of the vehicle. "Is she hurt?"

"I'm okay! I'm okay!" The woman released her hands and lifted them in the air. "Just scared out of my wits, is all." She shook her head slowly. "I thought my foot was on the brake, but it must have been on the gas pedal instead."

"I'll help you get her inside and then notify the sheriff about the accident," the other man said.

"Thanks, Dave." Ben introduced him to Elma; then he and Dave helped the woman from the vehicle while Elma retrieved her purse, which was lying in a heap on the floor of her car. Elma carried the purse as the men led the distraught woman into the store.

"There's a cot in the back room. Let's take her there so she can lie down." Elma wanted to be certain the woman really hadn't been injured. How thankful she was that no one else had been in the store when the accident occurred, especially outside near the wall where it had been pushed in.

Lizzie walked ahead of them. "I'll get things ready for her."

Once they had the woman situated on the cot, Ben went back outside. Like a mother hen, Lizzie fussed over the woman, while Elma handed the purse to her, asked her name, and whether there was anyone she would like to have notified of the accident.

"My name's Opal Freemont, and my daughter lives in the little town of Emma." She gave Elma the phone number, and while Lizzie gave Opal something cold to drink, Elma hurried outside.

As she neared the phone shack, her twin arrived, breathing heavily. "I heard a crash. What happened? Was anyone hurt?" Thelma's blue eyes widened when she looked at the car up against the building.

"The driver of the car is Opal Freemont, but she only seems to be shaken up." Elma took a breath. "Opal is in our back room, lying on a cot to rest. Lizzie is there, keeping her company." She adjusted her loosened head covering.

"I'm relieved to hear she's okay. I was on my front porch reading when the noise from the crash startled me." Thelma gave her sister a hug. "Do you need my help with anything?"

"You can sit behind the counter to wait on customers while I make a phone call to Opal's daughter to let her know what happened."

"Okay, I'll see you back inside." As Thelma turned toward the store, Ben stepped up to Elma. "The sheriff is on his way."

"Good to hear. The woman's name is Opal, and she gave me her daughter's phone number. I need to call and let her know what happened to her mother." Elma hesitated. "Oh, and after checking Opal over, I'm pleased to say she doesn't seem to be hurt."

"Good to hear." Ben crossed his arms, leaning against the small wooden building. "I'll wait outside while you make the call."

⁓

Ben didn't want to keep his driver waiting any longer, but after seeing how shook up Elma was, he didn't want to leave her, either. Since he couldn't take her out to lunch today, he told Dave if he had someplace he needed to go, maybe he could come back in a few hours and pick him up.

"There's no place I need to be, but guess I could go see my friend in Shipshe for a while." Dave's arms hung loosely at his sides. "You have my cell number, so give me a call when you're ready to go home."

"Okay, thanks." Ben gave a wave and watched as his driver turned his truck around and left the yard. Then he headed back to inspect the damage the car had done to the store.

Ben felt fortunate to have Dave as his main driver. One would never know this calm-talking man held a senior executive position for a well-known company for more than twenty years. But as Dave explained when they'd first met, all the money in the world meant nothing if a person wasn't happy with what he did. Dave told Ben being vice president of the company had been exciting at first, and he was getting paid more money than he knew what to do with, but after a few years, he got burned out, and the job he'd once loved ended up being something he dreaded.

Ben couldn't imagine waking up and going to a job he detested every day. He enjoyed his job of shoeing horses, and had met many nice people in the process.

A few minutes after Ben finished looking over the damage to the store, Elma stepped out of the phone shack, halting his thoughts.

"Opal's daughter is on her way." She glanced around. "Where'd your driver go?"

"He went to Shipshewana to see a friend. He'll be back later to get me."

Elma nodded her head.

After a bit of silence, Ben spoke again. "I had a chance to look over the damage to the store's basement wall."

"How bad is it?" Elma squinted her eyes with a look of dread.

"Some fixing needs to be done, but I think the sound of the crash was worse than the actual damage. Opal's car nudged the support beam in the corner of that wall pretty good, and I noticed a small crack in the beam, but it seems to be holding, at least for the time being." He rubbed his chin. "I wouldn't wait too long, though, to get it fixed."

"Okay. I know someone who'll probably come over right away to fix it for me." Elma looked at Ben with those pretty blue eyes, and his heart nearly melted. "Danki, Ben, for assessing the damage." She paused and released a long sigh. "Why don't you come inside? It's much too hot out here. Besides, Lizzie made a fresh peach pie, and I think we're all deserving of a piece."

"Sounds good to me." Ben followed Elma into the store. This wasn't the way he'd planned for the day to go, but at least he could spend some time with her. For that much he was grateful. Maybe next time he came to Topeka he could take her out for a meal.

∽

Grabill

Dorothy glanced out the kitchen window, then at the clock on the far wall. It was almost four o'clock, and still no Ben. *I wonder what could be keeping him.* When he left with Dave, he'd said he had some errands to run but hadn't said how long he would be.

She turned from the table and sat down with a huff. *I hope he's here in time for supper. Maybe I should go out to the phone shack and see if he called and left a message. I'd hate to start cooking supper and then end up eating by myself.*

She glanced at the clock one more time then rose to her feet.

Outside, Dorothy paused to look at her garden. Several mums had begun to bloom, and there were a few remaining daisies, but the lovely roses were what caught her eye. There were red, yellow, white, and pink ones, too.

Dorothy bent to sniff their aroma and drew in a lingering breath. She'd miss the colorful flowers in her yard when winter set in, but for now, she would enjoy them to the fullest.

A hummingbird swooped past Dorothy's head as it hovered near one of the bright red blooms. It wouldn't be long and the tiny birds would be gone for the rest of the year.

Every season brought a new change, and at least here in Indiana, one could count on spring, summer, autumn, and winter. Each brought its own beauty. What concerned Dorothy the most were the things she couldn't count on. One of those involved Ben. What if he never found a wife? Would he be content to continue living here and seeing to his mother's needs until the day she died? If he ended up marrying Martha or some other woman in the area, would they buy a place of their own, or would his bride be willing to live here? There were many questions and so few answers.

Dorothy needed to trust God and seek His will in all things, but it was difficult to do at times. She thought about the words to Isaiah 26:3: *"Thou wilt keep him in perfect peace, whose mind is stayed on thee."* If she kept her mind on Jesus and not circumstances, she would feel more peace.

As she headed for the phone shack, Dorothy prayed for peace. She was halfway down the path when Dave's truck pulled in. Ben got out, waved good-bye to Dave, and gave Dorothy a hug.

"How'd your day go, son? Did you get all your errands run?"

"My day turned out much different than I'd planned." He gestured toward the house. "Let's go inside and I'll tell you about it."

CHAPTER 18

Topeka

After Elma finished breakfast, she kept an eye on the clock. The vet would be by to check on Pearl's progress soon. The horse had been on antibiotics, along with salve to heal the nasty gash on her back leg. The veterinarian wanted to give the horse a couple of more weeks to improve and had been coming by regularly to check on her. Pearl's appetite was good, and the mare appeared to be getting back to her old self. Elma was glad to see her coming along so well. It would be nice to use Pearl again, even though Rusty wasn't so bad.

Since Elma still had time before the vet showed up, she took out some furniture polish and a rag to dust the living-room furniture. Once she finished, she picked up all the throw rugs and took them outdoors to shake and air on the line.

Elma was getting ready to return to the house when the veterinarian's truck pulled up by the barn. She hurried out to meet him. They engaged in conversation before going inside the barn to check Pearl's wound.

"You've done well taking care of your horse. The wound is healing like it should." He rubbed and patted the horse's side. "You're doing well, Pearl, but you'll need to be reshod pretty soon." The vet pointed to her hooves.

"When do you think it'll be safe for me to take her out on the road again?" Elma questioned.

"Since you have another buggy horse, you should give this one a little more time to heal. We don't want her to bump that wound and undo the progress she's made. I'd say another week or two, but use your discretion. Also, remember, she's an older horse and probably would like some time off."

Elma nodded. "You're right. Pearl's been around awhile. Maybe retirement isn't too far off in her future."

⁓

It had been two weeks since Opal Freemont's car hit the store, but thanks to Delbert and his friend Sam, who did masonry work, the repairs were finished and a new support post had been set in place. Fortunately, Opal's insurance paid for the damages to her car, and she'd given Elma money to pay for the work that needed to be done to the store. One good thing came from the accident, though. Ben had been calling Elma every few days to see how she was doing and hear the progress on the repairs.

Thinking about his most recent call, inviting her to go out to supper with him this evening, caused Elma's heartbeat to quicken.

She looked down at her fingernails and couldn't believe how rough they'd gotten. Elma wanted to make a nice impression on Ben—especially since this was their first real date. She went to her dresser and found an emery board and some hand lotion. Then she took a seat on the end of her bed and filed each nail until it had a nice rounded edge. After that, she worked with diligence, using the two-sided board to add a smooth, shiny surface to them. Satisfied that they looked better, she picked up her manicure kit and returned it to the dresser.

Glancing at the clock on the small table by her bed, she saw that it was five thirty, which meant Ben should be here within the next half hour. In some ways Elma wished Thelma and Joseph were going out with them. That way she'd have someone to talk to if the conversation lagged. But Ben hadn't suggested it, and it wasn't Elma's place to invite her sister and brother-in-law, so she would try to relax and think of enough things to talk about. With Ben hiring a driver to take them to and from the restaurant, it was almost like having a chaperone. If they couldn't think of anything to talk about during the drive, maybe Ben's driver would fill in the gaps. All she had to worry about was thinking of something to talk about during their meal at the restaurant.

Elma moved to stand in front of her dresser mirror, making sure her head covering was on straight and positioned correctly. She'd chosen to wear her lavender dress with matching cape and apron, since Thelma had said Elma looked good in that color. It was vain to think such thoughts, but she hoped Ben would appreciate the color of the dress and maybe even think she looked attractive.

Elma fanned her face. Was it the summer heat or being anxious to see Ben that made her cheeks flush? "Probably a little of both, don't ya think?" Elma directed her question to Freckles.

Cocking his head to one side, with ears perked, she almost felt as if the dog understood what she'd said.

When Elma heard the crunch of loose gravel from a vehicle pulling in, she peeked out her bedroom window. Instead of a truck, like the one Ben's driver had driven when he brought Ben to the store two weeks ago, she saw a minivan pulling into the yard. Either Dave had more than one vehicle, or Ben had hired someone else to bring him there this evening.

"Some watchdog you are," Elma said, nearly tripping over Freckles, who now lay in the hall outside her bedroom. He hadn't even barked. "Well, it doesn't matter. My ride is here, and you, my furry friend, must go down to the basement." With the August heat and humidity, Freckles would be in a cool, comfortable place for the evening.

Elma opened the basement door, and the dog went obediently down the stairs. She still couldn't get over how well–behaved this animal was. His previous master must have trained the dog well. She appreciated Freckles and felt thankful he'd come into her life at just the right time. Having the dog in the house during the night made her feel secure and a lot less lonely.

Elma shut the basement door, grabbed her black handbag, and hurried out the door. She met Ben as he came up the walk.

"I planned on coming up to the house to get you." Shoulders back, he held his head erect, never breaking his gaze into her eyes. "It's good to see you again, Elma."

She swallowed hard, clutching her purse against her side. "It's good to see you, too."

"I talked my favorite driver into driving his van tonight." Ben started walking in the direction of the vehicle. "Figured it'd be more comfortable for you, and we can sit in the back and visit without Dave feeling like he has to be part of the conversation."

"I see. I hope he won't think we're being rude if we don't include him."

Ben shook his head. "Nope. I've gotten to know Dave real well, and he's not the least bit sensitive. Nothing ruffles him."

"Okay."

Ben opened the passenger's door in the back, and Elma slid in. Then he went around to the other side and took his seat.

"It's nice to see you, Elma." Dave turned and smiled at her.

"Nice to see you, too. The seats in your minivan are comfortable."

He gave a nod. "This is really my wife's rig, but she lets me drive it whenever I need to."

"It's cool in here, too," Elma commented.

"If you like, I can turn the air-conditioning off or down, but I thought it would be more comfortable with this heat," Dave offered.

"No, you don't have to. It actually feels quite good." Elma was thankful for the cooling system in Dave's van. At least it would help to keep her from perspiring, since she was a ball of nerves.

"Okay, then." Dave turned around and pulled out of the driveway.

"You look nice in that color." Ben's cheeks colored as he looked at Elma.

"Danki."

"Are you hungerich?"

"I'm getting there. Where are we going?" Elma asked when Ben's driver headed out of Topeka in the direction of Shipshewana.

Ben grinned. "Thought we'd have supper at the Blue Gate Restaurant. Have you eaten there before?"

She nodded her head. "My sister and I ate there a few years ago." She saw no need to mention that it had been with Joseph and Delbert during the time the men had been courting the twins.

"They have good food at the Blue Gate," Dave interjected, glancing back at them from his rearview mirror. "My favorite supper dish there is meatloaf shepherd's pie. It's served with a generous helping of mashed potatoes smothered in a tasty blend of cheeses." He snickered. "Course, the smoked pork chops are real good, too."

"I may have to try the shepherd's pie." Elma looked at Ben. "What's your favorite meal?"

Ben smacked his lips as he gave his stomach a tap. "Anything that includes chicken. I like it fried, baked, or roasted."

"I like chicken, too," Elma agreed.

"Well, then, you're both in luck. The Blue Gate has plenty of chicken dishes on the menu," Dave called over his shoulder.

Elma shifted in her seat, pulling on the seat belt buckle to make sure it was snug enough. She always felt safe when she buckled herself in. Elma sometimes wished there were seat belts in Amish buggies. Wearing one kept a person from being jostled around, not to mention being safer in the event of an accident.

"See that crossroad over there?" Ben pointed to his left.

Elma nodded.

"It leads to an Amish-run business I'd like to visit someday—Lambright Wind Chimes."

"I've never been there, but my brother-in-law, Joseph, bought one of the Lambright chimes to hang in their backyard. It has a beautiful, melodic sound." Elma leaned against the seat, feeling quite relaxed. So far things were going well between her and Ben.

"I bet it does. The hardware store in Shipshe sells them, and after listening to the quality of their tinkling sound, I became interested." Ben reached across the seat and touched her arm. "Maybe the two of us can go there sometime."

"To the hardware store?" His touch had Elma feeling so rattled she could barely think or speak.

"No, to see where Lambright's chimes are made."

"Oh." Elma's cheeks warmed. She was sure they'd turned red, and she hoped Ben wouldn't notice. "That would be nice. I'd enjoy visiting there." She glanced his way.

Ben gave her a dimpled smile. "I'll be looking forward to it. Maybe we can do it soon, when we both have some time off from our jobs."

"Okay." Elma clasped her trembling hands together in her lap. *He wants to see me again. He must enjoy my company as much as I enjoy his. I'm already looking forward to seeing Ben again.*

⁓

"You're kind of fidgety tonight," Joseph commented as he took a seat beside Thelma on the couch. "Is the boppli kicking again and making you feel uncomfortable?"

"No, it's not the baby."

"Well, that's good." Joseph picked up a book to read. "Oh, I wanted to ask if you've been hungry for fish."

"I can always eat fish—fried or on the grill. Why? What were you thinking?"

"It's been a while since Delbert and I went fishing, and I'd like to check out the Little Elkhart River not far from here, where there's a designated trout stream. It feeds into a chain of lakes, which might be a nice area for all of us to go sometime. Maybe we could pack a picnic lunch and spend the afternoon there."

"Sounds nice, and I could surely eat some fresh trout." Thelma smiled. "Maybe we can have another cookout with Elma and Delbert—if you guys catch enough fish, that is." She poked Joseph in the ribs. Then just as quickly, she returned to her knitting and grew quiet.

"I'm sure Dell and I will bring home plenty for a supper meal." Joseph nudged Thelma's arm when she didn't respond. "Hey, all of a sudden you're like a million miles away. What's up?"

"I can't stop thinking about Elma."

"What about her?"

"She went out to supper with that Amish man from Grabill."

"You mean Ben Wagler?"

"Jah." Thelma's knitting needles clicked as she set them aside once more. "He's been calling her a lot lately, and now Ben's hired a driver to bring him all the way up here to take Elma to a restaurant." She pursed her lips. "He is moving way too fast, don't you think?"

Joseph shrugged his shoulders. "If a man knows what—or should

I say who—he wants, shouldn't he go after her? After all, Ben and Elma aren't getting any younger, so what's the point in wasting time? And look at us. . .it didn't take long for you and me to realize how we felt about each other."

"That part's true." Thelma gave her husband's arm a light tap, while her shoulders tightened. "They're not that old. But I don't want my *schweschder* to get hurt."

"Why would you think your sister's going to get hurt?" Joseph's chin jutted out.

"Ben lives in Grabill, and Elma lives here. It's a long-distance relationship, Joseph, and I don't see how it can work." Thelma peered at him over the top of the glasses she wore for reading and close-up work. "If they became serious about each other, one of them would have to move."

"Oh, I see what this is about." Joseph's eyes narrowed. "You're worried your sister might move to Grabill."

She nodded. "I couldn't stand it if Elma moved away. Until I married you, she and I always lived together. I'm thankful our home is across the street from hers so we can see each other regularly."

Joseph took hold of Thelma's hand and gave her fingers a tender squeeze. "I think you're worried about nothing. First of all, Ben and Elma don't know each other well enough to be making any kind of long-term commitment. And second, have you forgotten that the relationship between Elma and Delbert's cousin didn't last? One of the reasons was because Myron lived too far from Topeka and they rarely saw each other."

"True. Danki for reminding me." Thelma grasped her knitting needles once again. *Maybe Joseph is right. This whole thing with Elma and Ben could be just a passing fancy. I certainly hope that's the case, because I couldn't stand it if my twin sister moved away. I need her living close to me.*

CHAPTER 19

"Danki for helping me paint the boppli's room." Thelma gave her sister a hug.

"You're welcome. I'm glad I found the time to do it." Between work at the store and being courted by Ben, Elma's days were busier than ever.

Thelma opened the refrigerator and took out a pitcher of lemonade while Elma finished making tuna-salad sandwiches. "Why don't we take our lunch outside on the front porch?" Thelma suggested.

"Good idea. The fresh air will do us both some good."

Once outdoors, they took seats and bowed their heads for silent prayer. When they opened their eyes, Thelma handed Elma her sandwich and beverage.

As Elma ate and drank, she thought about how nice it was on this lovely September day, enjoying some quality time with her twin as she listened to the sounds of cows mooing in the distance. They both waved when a friend from their church district passed by in a buggy. Joseph and Thelma's porch gave a nice vantage point, enabling them to see a good ways down the road.

A slight breeze kicked up, and the wind chimes swayed with the harmony of soft, tinkling sounds.

"Those chimes sound so pretty." Elma cocked her head to listen.

"I know. I'm so glad Joseph moved them to the front porch for me. It seems lately I've been sitting out here a lot more." Thelma sighed.

"Ben wants to take me to an Amish-run business where they sell the Lambright wind chimes." Elma added. "I can't see the road from my house as well as you can, but I wouldn't mind having some wind chimes on my porch, too."

Thelma nodded but didn't respond to what Elma said about Ben. "I never grow tired of sitting out here and watching the people go by. Sometimes I bring my mending or knitting, but it's easy to lose track of time." Thelma drank the rest of her lemonade.

Elma bobbed her head. "I know what you mean. Wish I had my crossword-puzzle book with me."

They sat quietly for a while as Elma watched one of the sociable barn cats Thelma had named Marble come up to the porch. Meowing, it slunk over to them and jumped into Elma's lap. She set her empty plate on the wicker table and stroked the cat's silky head.

Thelma chuckled. "I remember when you wouldn't let any of the *katze* do that."

Elma shrugged. "I still prefer dogs, but cats do have an appeal, and they're good for keeping the mice at bay."

"I'll take the dishes inside while you enjoy sitting here with Marble."

"She's a pretty little calico, and her name always makes me think of Grandpa and Grandma Hochstetler. Remember the jar of marbles spilling when I had that nasty migraine a few years ago?" Smiling, Elma stared at the home across the street that had once been their precious grandparents'.

"I'll never forget that incident. I make sure the jar I keep full of Grandpa's marbles in the center of my kitchen table has a tight-fitting lid. Sure wouldn't want it getting tipped over and spilling all over the place like they did that day." Thelma collected the plates before going inside.

꙳

Grabill

Over the past several weeks, Ben had seen Elma as often as he could. He took her out to supper several times and joined Elma at her sister's house for pizza and games. The trips to and from Topeka were costing him money, but he didn't care. It was worth every penny to be able to spend time with her. By the middle of September, Ben was convinced he'd fallen in love with Elma. It might seem too soon to some people—especially Mom—but Ben knew what he wanted. Elma Hochstetler was the woman he'd been waiting for all his life. Of course, he hadn't told her yet. It might seem too forward, and the last thing he wanted to do was scare her off.

Ben had been invited to join Elma at her sister and brother-in-law's place tonight for a barbecue. He looked forward to going and was eager to get on with his day of shoeing several horses so he could rush back home and get ready for his driver to pick him up.

"Will you be leaving for work soon?" Mom asked when Ben placed his empty coffee cup in the sink.

"Jah. I've gotta get going so I'm home on time to get ready for my evening with Elma." His face broke into a wide smile.

Mom's gaze flitted around the room as she rubbed the side of her cheek. "You've been seeing her a lot lately."

He nodded. "I enjoy Elma's company. We have a lot in common."

Her forehead wrinkled. "Such as?"

"For one thing, we both like chicken as well as some other foods."

"*Puh!* You can't base a relationship on liking the same kind of food. You need to think alike on many levels, and—"

"Sorry." Ben held up his hand. "Can we talk about this some other time? If I don't go now, it'll take all day to get the horses done."

"Okay, I understand."

Ben picked up his lunch box and moved toward the door. "See you later, Mom. I hope you have a good day." By the time the door closed, he'd begun to whistle.

～

Groaning, Dorothy grabbed her cup of tea and sank into a seat at the table. If she didn't do something soon, she could very well lose her son to that young woman.

She took a sip of mint tea and let it roll around on her tongue as she thought things through. *I might be worried for nothing. It's not as if Ben is making plans to get married. I'm sure he'd tell me if he was. Maybe after he's courted Elma awhile and gotten to know her better, Ben will decide she's not the right woman for him.*

Dorothy sighed. She'd been convinced Martha was the right choice for Ben, but it didn't appear that he had any interest in the young woman. For that matter, Martha didn't seem too upset when word got out in their community that Ben had begun courting a woman from Topeka.

Doesn't anyone but me care that he might move away? If he did move, would he invite me to go with him? Is there any chance at all that Elma would be willing to move here?

She stared into her cup as her mouth twisted grimly. *No way could I leave my home. And if Ben left, it would mean he'd have to start all over with his business, looking for new clients who live in or close to Topeka.*

Dorothy turned and glanced at the throw rug by the back door where Hunter used to lie. It was a shame he never made his way back home. If Ben had his dog right now, maybe he'd be too busy getting him ready for the hunting season to worry about courting.

Topeka

Elma stood at her bathroom sink, patting her hot cheeks with cold water from the faucet. For the middle of September, it was still quite warm and humid. She wondered how much longer the hot weather would last. It was a good thing Joseph and Thelma's backyard had several shade trees. It would be much cooler eating out there at the picnic table than inside the warm house.

Elma wanted to have Ben over for a meal at her house but didn't feel it would be appropriate unless Joseph and Thelma joined them. Maybe in a few weeks she would invite them all over for an evening of homemade pizza and board games.

The more Elma saw Ben and talked with him on the phone, the more she liked him. She often caught herself fantasizing about what it would be like if she were married to him. If their relationship continued and Ben eventually proposed, she couldn't imagine herself saying anything but yes. After the wedding, Ben would need to move to Topeka, of course. Elma couldn't leave her sister—especially since Thelma was expecting a baby. Elma looked forward to being an aunt and helping her twin in any way she could.

Then there was the matter of running the store their grandparents had left them. Once the baby came, Thelma could not run the business by herself.

"And she shouldn't be expected to, either," Elma murmured. Owning the store and running it was a joint effort, and Elma wouldn't think of leaving her sister with the full responsibility.

Feeling flushed, Elma patted her cheeks with a little more cool water. *I don't know why I'm even thinking about all this. Even if Ben should propose, it won't be for a while, so there's no point in me dwelling on this right now.*

After brushing her teeth and making sure her hair was neatly combed with her bun and white head covering in place, Elma left the bathroom. When she stepped into the kitchen to get the healthy dessert she would take to Thelma's, she halted. Lying on the braided throw rug in front of the sink was Freckles, with Tiger nestled right beside him.

Elma grinned. "Amazing! I believe these two animals have actually become friends." She hated to disturb them, but it was time to leave, and Freckles needed to go down to the basement.

Well, maybe it wouldn't hurt this one time if she let him stay in the house. She wouldn't be gone more than a few hours, and if the cat and dog kept sleeping peacefully, everything should be fine.

CHAPTER 20

When Ben's driver dropped him off at Elma's house, he was pleased and yet a bit disappointed to see her waiting for him on the front porch. He'd sort of hoped he might get to see the inside of her house, since he was curious if she kept it as neat as she did the store. Well, maybe some other time. Right now, he looked forward to spending the evening with Elma and getting to know her sister and brother-in-law better.

"Guder owed." Ben stepped onto the porch and offered her what he hoped was his best smile.

"Good evening." Elma's lips parted slightly as he took her hand, giving her fingers a gentle squeeze. What Ben really wanted to do was hug her, but he didn't want to appear too forward. Besides, Elma's sister might be watching from across the street.

"Are you ready to go?" he asked.

"Jah. I just need to get the dessert I'm taking." She gestured to the cardboard box sitting on the small table near the porch swing.

"I'll carry it for you." Ben picked up the box and stepped off the porch.

"Danki."

As Ben walked beside Elma, his thoughts ran wild. It was too soon to be thinking such things, but he couldn't help picturing her as his bride. *If we got married, would she be willing to move to Grabill? If we had children, would they resemble her or take after me?*

As they paused at the end of the driveway to look for oncoming cars, Ben looked at Elma and smiled. "How was your day?"

"It went well. Not quite so busy at the store, so it gave me a chance to do some organizing." She laughed. "Of course, that kind of work can be tiring, too."

"You're right. From what I've seen of your store, it looks pretty well organized." While holding the dessert box in one hand, it felt right resting his other hand on the small of Elma's back as he escorted her across the road.

Elma waited until they'd crossed the street to reply. "I try to keep things put in their proper place, but with people coming and going and handling various items, the shelves can get a bit messy at times." She paused when they reached her sister's driveway. "Running the store is a full-time job, and with Thelma only working part-time, I couldn't do it all without Lizzie's help."

He nodded. "I don't have anyone helping me shoe horses, but there are several good neighbors I can call on when it's time to harvest our fields."

"You must keep quite busy. I'm surprised you've been able to take the time to come here for visits."

"To see you, I'm more than happy to take some time off." An empty feeling came over Ben when he dropped his hand from her back.

A blotch of red erupted on Elma's cheeks. "That's nice to hear, but I hope you're not setting your work aside on my account."

"Nope. I've planned my schedule around trips up here."

She slackened her pace and looked up at him. "Thelma and I took some time out to paint the nursery for the up-and-coming arrival."

"I'll bet it looks nice." He slowed his steps to match hers.

"Jah. The nursery will be cute with all the baby's things in it."

"I've always wanted kinner."

"Same here." Elma's cheeks reddened further.

As they continued their leisurely walk toward the house, a beautiful golden retriever pranced down the driveway to greet them, barking and wagging its tail.

"This is Joseph's dog, Ginger." Elma bent down to pat the dog's head.

"She's a good-looking hund. Do you have any pets, Elma?"

"Jah. I have a cat named Tiger, and a dog I call Freckles."

He tipped his head. "I'm surprised I haven't seen either one whenever I've dropped by the store or come to pick you up."

"Tiger often hangs out in the barn during the day, and I keep Freckles in the basement when I'm going somewhere or at work in the store. I haven't had him very long, and don't want to chance him running off."

Ben shifted the box in his hands. "I understand. My dog, Hunter, ran off when I was delivering some of my mamm's flowers to a lady who lives in—"

"Welcome, Ben." Thelma joined them on the lawn and shook Ben's hand. "I see you've met my husband's hund."

He gave a nod. "She's a real beauty."

"She can also be a *pescht*." Thelma nudged the dog with her knee. "They've had enough greeting, Ginger. Now go lie down."

The dog slunk off with its tail between its legs and found a spot to lie down on the back porch.

"I brought some dessert." Elma took the box from Ben. "Should I take it to the kitchen, Thelma?"

"Please do, and I'll go with you, since I still have a few more things to bring out to the picnic table." Thelma smiled at Ben. "Joseph's grilling steaks on the barbecue." She pointed in that direction. "Why don't you join him while Elma and I are in the kitchen? I realize you met my husband some time ago at the farmers' market, but it'll give you two a chance to get better acquainted."

"Okay, I'll do that." As the women headed into the house, Ben ambled across the yard to where Joseph stood in front of the barbecue grill.

⁓

"Your cheeks are flushed," Thelma commented when Elma placed her dessert on the counter.

Elma touched her face. "I suppose they would be since it's so hot outside. Seems like summer is going to carry right into fall this year."

"Jah, I expect it will." Thelma placed her hands on her well-rounded belly. "Sure hope things are cooler when the boppli comes toward the middle of October."

Elma clasped her sister's hands. "It's hard to believe you only have one month to go."

"I know." Thelma sighed. "I hope Mom and Dad can come for a visit soon after the boppli is born."

"I'm sure they will. After all, this is their first *kinskind*, so they'll be anxious to greet the little one." Elma opened the refrigerator door and took out a jug of iced tea. "Should I take this outside, along with a bucket of ice?" Her sister almost always served iced tea when they had a cookout.

"That'd be great, but could you wait a minute? There's something I'd like to talk to you about." Thelma took a seat at the kitchen table and motioned for Elma to do the same.

"What is it?" Elma asked after she'd pulled out a chair and sat down.

"It's about you and Ben." Thelma blew out a series of short breaths.

"What about us?"

"Are you two getting serious?"

"I'm not sure. Maybe. . . I think so. Why do you ask?"

Thelma's eyebrows rose as she touched the back of her neck. "I've seen the way Ben looks at you, and I am frightened."

"Why?"

"I don't want you to move away from me, Sister. I would be lost without you, and now, with the boppli coming, I'm going to need you even more."

Elma got up and went to stand beside Thelma's chair. "You needn't worry. I'm not going anywhere." She placed her hands on Thelma's shoulders. For the first time since Ben had been courting Elma, she realized their relationship couldn't go any further. If he were to propose marriage someday, she would have to say no, because she couldn't move to Grabill and leave her twin.

⌒

As Thelma watched her sister go out the door with the jug of iced tea, a lump formed in her throat. She hoped she hadn't said too much. Elma's heavy sigh and the downward tilt of her chin gave evidence of suppressed disappointment. She was clearly infatuated with Ben and perhaps even thought she was in love with him.

But Ben isn't the right man for Elma. He lives too far away and would most likely expect her to move to Grabill if they got married. It might be selfish, but I need Elma here with me—especially with the baby coming soon.

Thelma cupped her hand under her chin. *And who would run the store if my sister moved from Topeka? I certainly can't run it by myself, and it would be a shame to sell it.*

Thelma stared at the table, unsure of what to do. All the unknowns caused many questions to run through her head. She wanted her sister's happiness, but surely Elma could find contentment with some other man. *Is it wrong for me to depend on my sister because I'm having a baby?*

She glanced at the refrigerator, remembering that Joseph had gone fishing with Delbert last Saturday, and they still hadn't eaten the trout they'd caught that morning and later froze. Maybe what she ought to do was invite Elma and Delbert for a fish fry next week. Perhaps a bit more time spent with Joseph's good friend would open her sister's eyes.

⁓

Ben's excitement over being with Elma and her family fizzled a bit as the evening progressed. For some reason, Elma, who'd been friendly and talkative earlier, had become quiet, responding only when Ben asked a question, but no longer initiating a conversation of her own. Plus, she no longer looked at him—not even when he spoke to her. Ben was perplexed by this. He hoped he hadn't said or done something to embarrass or upset her.

But if so, what did I say? I've tried to be polite and friendly to Elma and her family. He shifted on the picnic bench. *Maybe Elma's tired from working at the store all day and it's caught up to her.*

Ben pulled out his pocket watch, noting the time. His driver would be back in an hour or so, picking him up over at Elma's place, where he'd dropped him off.

"Now that we're done eating, should we play a game of horseshoes while the women get dessert ready?" Joseph nudged Ben's arm.

Startled, Ben jumped. "Jah, sure, that'd be great. I can only play thirty minutes or so, though. My driver will pick me up in an hour, and I'll need a little time to walk Elma home."

Joseph's shoulders drooped; then he straightened them again. "Okay, guess thirty minutes is better than nothing." He got up from the bench and went to get out the horseshoes.

Ben and Joseph played, with Ginger yapping every time each of them took a turn, until Thelma called them back to the picnic table to eat Elma's dessert.

"You're a good cook, Elma." Ben wiped the crumbs off his face from the blueberry crisp. "This is sure tasty."

Elma smiled, although it didn't quite reach her eyes. "I got the recipe from a harvest cookbook and altered it a bit so it doesn't have cane sugar in it. It's also gluten-free."

Joseph smacked his lips. "Well, you did real good because I'd never know it was a healthy dessert if you hadn't just said so."

"Elma has always tried to get me, as well as others, to eat a healthier diet." Thelma passed around some napkins. "But I have to say, I appreciate it—especially after trying this appenditlich dessert."

Ben looked at Elma to see her response. She merely smiled at her sister and quietly said, "Danki."

By the time they finished dessert, Ben spotted his driver pulling his truck up Elma's driveway. Dave was either early, or Ben had lost track of time.

Ben threw his legs over the bench and stood. "I hate for the evening to end, but Elma, if you're ready to go, I'll walk you home now."

She glanced at her sister, and when Thelma nodded, Elma stood, too. "You can keep the dessert, Thelma." She gave her sister a hug, shook Joseph's hand, and headed down the driveway with Ben.

After crossing the street, and before approaching Dave's truck, Ben stopped walking and reached for Elma's hand. He was surprised at how cold it felt. Although the sun had begun to set, the air was still quite warm and humid. Compared to Elma's, Ben's hand seemed hot.

"I enjoyed being with you tonight," he whispered, bending close to her ear. "How would you like to come for supper at my house next Saturday? I can either have my driver pick you up, or if you prefer to have one of your drivers bring you to Grabill, I'll pay them for bringing you to my house."

Elma lowered her head a bit while clearing her throat. "Sorry, Ben, but I have plans for next Saturday."

"Oh." He couldn't hide his disappointment. "How about the Saturday after that?"

She stared down at her feet. "I'm not sure, Ben. Thelma's due to have her boppli sometime in October, and I need to be close so I'm available when it happens." She let go of his hand.

Already missing the feel of her soft skin, Ben slowly nodded. "Guess that makes sense. Well, I'll give you a call soon and see if we can work something out. Maybe I'll just come up this way again."

"All right, but please call before you come, okay?" Elma spoke so softly Ben could barely hear the words.

"I won't show up unless I've talked to you first." On impulse, Ben leaned down and gave her a quick kiss on the cheek. "*Gut nacht,* Elma."

"Good night, Ben."

As Ben got into Dave's truck a strange feeling came over him—a premonition of sorts. He couldn't be sure, but he was almost convinced something had happened tonight to make Elma pull away from him. He wished now he'd had the nerve to ask.

Chapter 21

Grabill

Shoulders slouched and head down, Ben stepped out of the phone shack. He'd left another message for Elma but didn't know why. He'd made several calls in the last three weeks, and she'd never called him back.

Jerking his hat off, he felt like throwing it on the ground. Instead, Ben ran his fingers through his hair. *I don't get it. Is there something wrong that she hasn't responded? Could Thelma have had her baby? If so, I would think Elma might have at least let me know.* Ben's jaw clenched as he leaned against the small building. *Maybe Elma doesn't want to see me anymore. She did act a bit strange when I walked her home after the cookout at her sister and brother-in-law's place. Sure hope I didn't do anything to mess things up between us. I can't picture myself with anyone else but Elma.*

Ben's boots felt like they were full of lead. Every step took great effort as he made his way back to the house.

He found his mother in the kitchen, sitting at the table, reading her Bible. As he approached, she looked up and pointed to the coffeepot on the stove. "There's still plenty of kaffi left, if you'd like a second cup."

"Okay, it does sound good. Maybe it'll help me perk up."

"Are you feeling down this morning or just tired?"

"A little of both." Ben poured himself a cup of coffee and took a seat at the table across from her.

"Want to talk about it?"

He shook his head. A few days ago he'd mentioned not hearing from Elma, and Mom had said it might be for the best, since long-distance relationships were difficult. Ben hadn't wanted to hear that, so he decided not to mention it again—at least not to his mother.

"Do you have a full work schedule today?" Mom asked while fiddling with the pleats of her dark green dress.

"No, not really."

Ben's spoon clicked against the inside of his mug as he stirred his coffee. The last thing on his mind was work. *Elma is such a nice person. Maybe ignoring my phone messages is her way of telling me it's over—sort of softening the blow.* They'd had so little time together. A solid relationship had never really gotten off the ground. But how could it with so many miles between them? Despite it all, though, this was the first time Ben had ever felt serious about a woman. Like a wildfire, it happened so fast.

Pushing his thoughts aside, Ben glanced out the window. It was a beautiful morning and still quite warm, as it had been the last couple of weeks. He noticed droplets of dew on the grass, sparkling like diamonds as the sun cast light on the blades. Looking farther out in the fields, he noticed the patchy ground fog slowly ascending into the blue sky. Ben figured by midmorning the fog clouds would disperse and temperatures would rise with the heat of the glaring sun. It was unusual having such hot weather carry into fall. *Sure would be fun sitting on a porch swing with Elma, watching the morning unfold.* He drew in a breath and let out a heavy sigh.

"So what are your plans for the day?" Mom cleared her throat a couple of times. "Son, did you hear me?"

"Uh, sorry, guess my mind was wandering."

"I asked what your plans are for today."

"I have a horse to shoe, and there are a few things I probably should do around here before it gets too hot, but I think I'm gonna let 'em wait till tomorrow."

Mom's eyes narrowed. "You know what your daed would say about that."

"Jah. He'd say, 'Benjamin, you should never put off what you'd planned to do today till tomorrow, 'cause tomorrow might never come.'" Ben blew on his coffee and took a sip. "It's good advice, but sometimes plans change and things have to wait."

Mom lifted the bottom of her apron to fan her face. "Are you thinking of anything in particular?"

Ben shrugged as his mind drifted in another direction. He had to see Elma. Needed to know what was going on.

Setting his cup on the table, he got up, said good-bye to his mother, and hurried out the back door. *Sure hope one of our drivers is available to take me to Topeka this afternoon.*

∽

Topeka

"Joseph, it's time to go." Thelma nudged her husband's arm as he sat beside her at the breakfast table.

He looked at the clock on the kitchen wall and shook his head. "I don't have to head to the harness shop for at least another half hour."

"No, I mean it's time for us to go to the birthing center."

His eyes widened. "The b–boppli's coming?"

"Jah. I started having contractions during the night."

"Why didn't you wake me?"

"Because they weren't strong enough." Thelma grimaced as a sharp pain shot through her middle and around her back. "But they've gotten closer now."

Joseph leaped out of his chair, nearly knocking it to the floor. "I'd better call a driver. Can't take the chance of making the trip by horse and buggy." He paused and wiped his sweaty forehead. "We might not make it in time."

"Calm down and take a deep breath. I'm sure we'll be fine. But I agree, hiring a driver to take us there would be the best thing." Thelma pushed away from the table. "Oh, and after you do that, could you please run across the street and let Elma know? I want both you and her to be with me in the birthing room."

"Okay. You'd better go to the living room and lie on the couch till I get back." Joseph's face looked like all the blood had drained out. He grabbed his straw hat and rushed out the back door.

Thelma had already packed a small bag with the things she would need for herself and the baby, so all she had to do now was try to stay calm. With this being her first pregnancy, she couldn't help feeling some apprehension. Especially since the baby wasn't due for a couple of more weeks.

○ᗢ

Elma had just finished eating breakfast when someone knocked on the back door.

"Coming!" she called.

Woof! Woof! Elma's dog raced for the door.

"Calm down, Freckles, and let me see who's there." When Elma opened the door, she was surprised to see Joseph on the porch, lips pressed together while tugging on his right ear.

His strange behavior caused her concern. "What is it, Joe? Is everything all right? You look naerfich."

"I admit. I am feeling nervous right now."

"What's wrong?"

"It—it's Thelma." Joseph's knees bent, then straightened, as his brows pulled in. "The b–boppli's coming." The poor man could hardly manage to get the words out. Elma hadn't seen him this flustered since the day he married her sister. She understood how he felt, though, for she, too, felt naerfich right now.

"Already? B–but she's not due for two more weeks." Now Elma was the one stuttering. None of this seemed real. She felt as if she were in the middle of a dream.

"Maybe the doctor was wrong. Or perhaps the boppli decided to come early. Either way, your sister says it's time, and she wants you to go to the birthing center with us. I've already called our driver, and he's on his way right now." Joseph seemed more confident, as he puffed out his chest. "Just think, Elma, I'm about to become a daed, and you'll soon be our little one's aunt." His voice cracked. "I'm thankful my business has picked up, 'cause I have a family to care for."

Elma's mouth felt dry, and she licked her lips, hoping it might help. "It is hard to believe the day we've all been waiting for is finally here. Once the boppli makes his or her entrance into the world, none of our lives will ever be the same."

With a vigorous nod, Joseph turned to head back home. Walking backward, he hollered, "You will go with us to offer your sister support, won't ya?"

"Of course I'll go. Wild horses wouldn't keep me away. I'll be at your house lickety-split."

As she went about closing up the house, excitement welled in Elma's chest. This was the day they'd all been waiting for. She sent up a quick prayer. *Please Lord, let everything be all right—for my sister and her child.*

⌣

Grabill

Dorothy put a lid on the soup and took out the items needed to make sandwiches for when Ben arrived home for lunch. She had his routine down, and when Ben spent the morning with clients, he was always ready to eat when he got home.

Once the bread was toasted in the oven, Dorothy made a jug of iced tea. She was almost done slicing a lemon when Ben stepped in the door. He set his things down and tossed his hat on the wall peg.

"Hi, Mom. Something smells good." He took a seat by the back door and pulled off his new boots. "Ah, that feels better."

"It's never fun breaking in a pair of shoes or boots. You should do it in small phases." Dorothy removed the lid from the kettle. "I made chicken noodle soup, and I'll get us a couple fried–egg sandwiches started quickly."

Ben sat, rubbing the toes of his feet. "Okay."

"You can get washed up. It won't be long till lunch is ready." Dorothy watched her son get up from his chair and leave the room; then she turned to the stove and broke two extra-large eggs into the skillet. While they cooked, she dished up the hot soup and placed their bowls on the table.

By the time Ben returned, the sandwiches were ready, so they sat down and offered their silent prayers. Then Ben added several crackers to his soup and started in.

"Did you have a *gut mariye*?" Dorothy handed Ben his sandwich plate.

"My morning was as good as any other this week." Ben smacked his lips. "This soup is sure tasty, Mom."

"Danki. I'm glad you like it." Dorothy gestured to her bowl of soup. "I added more noodles than usual." She grabbed a napkin.

They ate in silence for a while, but Dorothy wanted some conversation. "I'll need to get some weeding done after lunch. I also have cherry tomatoes ripe enough for picking."

He nodded and continued eating.

Dorothy wondered if he had something on his mind. "Are you going back out to shoe more horses this afternoon?"

Ben glanced at the wall clock and shook his head.

Dorothy frowned. It felt as though she were having a one-way conversation.

"That was good, Mom." He stood and put his dirty dishes in the sink then sat back down to put on his boots.

"If you have no more horses to take care of, where are you going?"

"I have an errand to run, and I'd better get going. Danki for lunch. See you later."

When Ben headed out the door, grabbing his hat, Dorothy finished her meal then rose to tidy up the kitchen.

When her chore was done, she went outside and got down to business. Dorothy weeded awhile then collected an abundance of tomatoes and other vegetables. After bringing her produce inside and setting it on the table, she deposited the warm, fragrant tomatoes carefully into the sink. While rinsing them with cool water and placing each one on a towel to dry, her mind drifted.

It's strange that Ben hasn't mentioned his friend Elma the last few days. Could he be losing interest in her? Dorothy shifted her weight and kept rinsing the vegetables. *If so, it's for the best. He needs to find someone closer to home.*

Chapter 22

Topeka

When Ben stepped onto the porch of Elma and Thelma's store, he was surprised to see a Closed sign in the window. It was ten o'clock in the morning. The store should be open by now.

Ben sprinted back to his driver's vehicle. "The store's closed, so I need to head to Elma's house and see if she's there."

"Okay." Dave gave a nod. "I'll park my truck down by the house. Do you want to ride with me or walk over there?"

"I'll walk and meet you there." Instead of walking, however, Ben ran all the way to Elma's front door. His skin felt clammy and sweat trickled down his forehead, but he didn't care. Ben knocked several times. When no one answered, he ran around back and knocked on that door. Still no answer. The only thing he heard was the muffled sound of a dog barking. He stood listening a few seconds. It had to be his imagination, but the bark sounded familiar—almost like. . . *No, it couldn't be. That was Elma's dog, Freckles, barking.*

He stepped off the porch and ran back to Dave's truck. "Elma's not here, so I guess we oughta head back to Grabill." Groaning, he climbed into the passenger's side, wiping his face with a handkerchief.

"Maybe she's across the street at her sister's, where you had the cookout a few weeks ago." Dave turned on the air-conditioning. "If you want to check, I'll drive you over there."

"Good idea. If Elma's not there, maybe Thelma will know where she is." Ben rubbed a knot on the nape of his neck. "Sure hope everything's okay with her."

When they pulled into Joseph and Thelma's yard, Ben hopped

out of the truck and ran up to the house. He knocked on the front door several times, but nobody answered. Then he ran around back to see if anyone was in the yard. No one was in sight. After knocking on the back door with no luck, Ben returned to Dave's truck. "The Beechys aren't home, either. If you don't mind taking me to Elma's again, I'll leave a note on her door. Then we may as well head home."

༄

Elma stood on one side of Thelma, wiping her sister's forehead, while Joseph stood on the other, holding her hand and giving encouragement as Thelma pushed again.

Thelma had been laboring a couple of hours since they arrived at the birthing center, but now the pains were really intense.

"Why's it taking so long?" Thelma moaned, her face red from all the pushing.

"Our little one is just being stubborn." With a calm voice, Joseph grinned. "The boppli isn't even born yet, and it's already taking after me."

That got a quick chuckle out of Thelma before her face scrunched up and she bore down again.

Elma didn't say a whole lot. She let Joseph give her sister encouragement. Elma figured it helped him, too, because she knew how nervous he was. Elma wiped the cool cloth over her sister's brow again. Looking toward the other end of the bed, Elma realized she would soon be seeing her niece or nephew seconds after it came into the world.

Elma wished she could take the pain away from Thelma but was hopeful it wouldn't be much longer. She'd always heard labor pains were quick to be forgotten once the baby was put in its mother's arms. Despite the pain her sister was going through, Elma was glad to be present, watching this miracle unfold.

"All right now, the baby's coming. Bear down and give me one more good push," the midwife urged Thelma.

Elma instinctively took Thelma's other hand, while Joseph continued to hold her other.

Thelma took a deep breath, raised up, and pushed with all her might.

"It's a boy," the midwife proclaimed, "but lay back and relax a little, because you're not done."

Joseph's head jerked when his newborn son was placed into the nurse's arms, who had been standing by and assisting the midwife. "Wh–what do you mean?"

"Just relax, Joe," Elma spoke up. "She still has to deliver the afterbirth."

The midwife shook her head. "It's more than that. The monitor is indicating there's a second heartbeat."

"It has to be Thelma's heartbeat you're hearing." Joseph gave a nod. "Right?"

The midwife shook her head before examining Thelma further. "You know what? There's a second baby coming."

Joseph's eyes widened, while Elma and Thelma both gasped. "Twins?" they asked in unison.

"Yes. Now this could take some time, so just relax, Thelma. After this one is born, we will transfer you to the hospital so you and the babies can be checked out."

Thelma grunted. "It's not going to take any time at all. I need to push now."

Elma watched in amazement as, a few minutes later, a perfect baby girl made her entrance into the world. Tears welled in her eyes. What a joy to witness the miracle of her sister giving birth to not one, but two precious children. At the same time, Elma couldn't help feeling envious. She could only imagine the thrill of having a child of her own. *But it may never happen,* she reminded herself. *I need to be happy for Thelma and Joe and appreciate the joys of being an aunt.*

Elma bent close to her sister. "I'm going out to make a phone call. Mom and Dad need to know you've given birth to twins."

"Would you call my folks and leave a message for them, too?" Joseph looked tenderly at the infant cradled in his arms after the nurse cleaned the baby boy.

"Jah, of course, I'll make the call." Elma watched when the nurse finished cleaning their tiny girl and laid her gently into Thelma's arms.

Both Joseph and Thelma had tears in their eyes, as did Elma. Taking one last look at the happy family, she slipped quietly from the room.

◯

Thelma gazed at her twins in awe. "I had no idea there were two babies inside my womb. How come we never realized it?" she asked the nurse. "I mean, I never got that big, and no one ever said they heard two heartbeats."

The nurse pursed her lips. "We actually did hear two during your appointments, but we thought the second one was an echo of your heartbeat, because it was so faint. Also, since you didn't have an early ultrasound, the second baby was obviously hidden behind the first one."

"Guess that makes sense," Joseph put in. "Whew!" He blew out his breath in a loud puff. "Can you believe it, Thelma? We have a *bu* and a *maedel*. What are we gonna name them?"

"I don't know, but we need to make a decision soon." Thelma blinked as tears seeped out from under her lashes. "Maybe when Elma gets back from making the phone calls."

"The babies' names can be decided later," the nurse said. "The first thing we need to do is get you and the twins transferred to the hospital."

Thelma swallowed hard. From what she could tell, her son and daughter looked perfect. She hoped and prayed they would be pronounced healthy, and they could all go home soon.

◯

Elma stood in the hallway outside her sister's room after calling her parents, as well as Joseph's folks, to share the good news. She'd left messages for both couples since no one was in their phone shacks when she called.

She leaned against the wall, goose bumps erupting on her arms. *It's really happened. Thelma is officially a mamm, and I'm those precious babies' aendi. It's amazing how one's life can change in a single day. How wunderbaar to see our family growing. Someday, the children will be grown and getting married. Then I'll have the opportunity of being a great-aunt.*

Elma closed her eyes. *Thank You, Lord, for giving my sister and her husband two babies to love and cherish. I pray when they get to the hospital, the doctor will pronounce them both perfectly healthy. Help me to find the time to be there for Thelma when she needs me the most. Thank You again, for all that You do. Amen.*

Chapter 23

Elma sat in her sister's rocking chair, tears welling in her eyes as she gazed at the precious baby girl in her arms. It had been a week since Thelma's twins were born, and she'd taken time off from working at the store to help out. Mom and Dad hadn't come to see the babies yet, because Mom had been down with a bad cold. But she was better now, and they'd be arriving sometime today. Once they got settled in, Mom would take care of Thelma and the babies so Elma could open the store again. Elma had thought about letting Lizzie run the place in her absence but figured that wouldn't go well, so closing it for a week had seemed like the logical thing to do.

"Looks like you've put Miriam to sleep." Thelma snuggled her son in her arms. "Charles is sleeping, too."

Elma smiled. "Jah." She was pleased Joseph and Thelma chose to name their daughter after their grandma Miriam, and their son after Joseph's grandfather, Charles. It was an honor for the children to be named after a relative.

Elma stroked Miriam's soft cheek. *If I ever have a daughter I'll call her Kathryn, after my mamm. And if I had a son. . .*

A vision of Ben popped into Elma's head, as she thought about the note he'd left on her door the day the twins were born. She was sorry she had missed him, but it was probably for the best.

If I were married to Ben, what name would he choose for our son? Elma leaned her head against the back of the chair and closed her eyes. There was no point thinking about this. She and Ben were not getting married, and unless she found someone who lived closer, it wasn't likely she'd ever get married.

During the last three weeks, Ben had left messages for Elma on her voice mail, but she'd been too busy to respond—first at the store, and then helping Thelma.

I ought to call him. At least let him know Thelma had her babies and that I'm too busy to see him right now. Perhaps in time, Ben will give up on our relationship and stop calling. It would be easier than having to tell him the reason I've pulled away.

"I hear a vehicle pulling in." Thelma's eyes brightened. "I bet it's Mom and Dad with their driver."

⌒

Grabill

After Ben finished with his last client for the day, he stopped at a grocery store to grab a snack. He needed some energy to get him going again.

Ben chatted with the clerk a few minutes, paid for the items, and left the building. He went back to his buggy and sat munching on an apple, while watching customers come and go from the store. When he finished his snack, he tossed the core and the empty water bottle into the nearest trash can.

He walked over to the hitching rail and stood there, thinking about Elma, as he so often did these days. *I wonder why she hasn't returned any of my calls. Sure hope the last time we were together I didn't do something to offend her.*

Over and over he had relived the evening they were at Thelma and Joseph's. Ben remembered every word spoken between him and Elma but could not come up with anything that might have upset her. He remembered how his heart skipped a beat when he guided Elma across the road, and the way she looked at him when they talked earlier in the evening. But then something had changed in her demeanor, and she'd said very little. It was as though she'd lost interest or was preoccupied.

Forcing his thoughts aside, Ben untied his horse and paused to give him a few pats. Then he climbed into the buggy and backed up his rig before heading onto the street.

A short ways down the road, Fella threw a shoe. "Oh, great, just what I don't need today. It's like the story of the shoemaker—always too busy taking care of everyone else to notice his children were going without good shoes." Ben clucked to his horse. "Don't worry, boy. We'll take it easy on the way home. I'll get you fixed up soon."

⁓

"Look what I got while you were working today." Ben's mother grinned when he entered the kitchen, as she sat in a chair, holding a black-and-tan German shorthair puppy. "I know how much you miss Hunter, so I thought you'd like to have this cute little fella."

Ben glanced at the pup then looked away. "I appreciate the thought, but I'm not interested, Mom. No hund could ever replace the one I lost."

"Of course not, but you may end up liking this dog as much as you did Hunter." She stroked the puppy's ears. "Isn't he the cutest thing? And look how relaxed he is in my arms. Would you like to hold him?"

Ben shook his head. "He seems nice enough, but I don't want another dog." He placed his lunch box on the counter and got a drink of water. "Since you like the hund so much, he can be yours."

Her lips compressed. "But I got him for you, Ben."

He gripped his glass of water. Didn't his mother get it? Why was it so hard for her to understand?

"Any thoughts on what name the dog should have?"

He shrugged. "Whatever you want to call him is fine by me. He'll be with you most of the time anyway, so you ought to choose the name."

Rocking from side to side in her chair, almost as if she were keeping time to some unheard music, Mom smiled and said, "How about Partner? A good hunting dog should be the hunter's partner, don't you think?" With that, the puppy barked and licked Mom's nose. "Ah, you are such a cute little baby. He likes his new name." Mom cooed and continued to cuddle the puppy.

"I suppose." It was all Ben could do to keep from rolling his eyes. Mom was already stuck on this dog, and to make matters worse, she expected him to be, too. Well, she could keep the mutt if she wanted, and if it made her feel better, Ben would let her think he'd accepted the animal, too. It was better to go along with things than stir up a problem.

"What time's supper?" Ben asked, setting his empty glass in the sink.

"Not for another half hour or so."

"Good. It gives me time to go out and replace my horse's lost shoe. When I come back I can eat, take a shower, and change into clean clothes."

"Sorry to hear your gaul lost his shoe, but at least you can remedy the problem." Mom smiled, nuzzling the pup's head.

"It's true, but it only lengthens my workday. I didn't check the phone messages coming home today. Did I have any calls?" Ben crossed his arms.

"Only one. It was from a customer, confirming their eight o'clock appointment tomorrow morning."

"Okay, thanks." Out of respect for Mom, Ben leaned down and gave the dog a pat on the head. He had to admit, the pup was sweet. And who could resist a puppy? The animal responded by licking Ben's hand as he started to move it away.

Mom smiled up at him. "See there. . . Already, Partner likes you."

"Jah, I suppose." Ben shuffled back outside and headed for the barn. Shaking his head, he couldn't help thinking, *If I don't watch out, that dog is gonna grab at my heartstrings.*

Speaking of heartstrings. . . As he approached the barn door, a vision of Elma popped into Ben's head. *Since she still hasn't returned any of my calls, if I don't hear something from her by tomorrow, I'm gonna hire Dave to take me to Topeka so I can find out for myself if anything is wrong.*

᭜

Topeka

"Such a *siess* little maedel. Oh, and I love the name you chose for your daughter," Mom said when Thelma handed Miriam to her.

Tears gathered in Mom's eyes as she stroked the top of her

granddaughter's head. "I can't get over all her pretty auburn hair."

Joseph grinned. "Yep. She takes after her daed." He gestured to little Charles, being held by Thelma's father. "Can't tell for sure yet, 'cause it's kinda sparse, but it looks like he may have his mamm's brown hair."

Thelma smiled. It was good to have her folks here, making a fuss over the twins and offering their help, but she couldn't help noticing the look of longing on her sister's face. If only Elma were married and had a baby. Thelma was certain Elma had felt left out when she and Joseph got married. Now, becoming a parent was one more thing she and Elma couldn't share. It didn't seem fair that her twin had no husband. Up until Thelma fell in love with Joseph and they decided to get married, she and Elma had done everything together. Truth was, they'd made a promise to each other many years ago that neither of them would marry unless the other one did. Of course, Elma had relinquished Thelma from her promise, saying she wanted her sister's happiness and wouldn't hold her back. Thelma was so deliriously happy on her wedding day, she hadn't stopped to truly consider her twin's feelings.

"Have many visitors come to see the new bopplin so far?" Mom looked at Thelma.

"Jah, we've had some from church, and a couple of neighbors stopped in." Thelma sat back in her seat. "It's been a busy week since we brought the babies home."

"Have you had anyone from any distance come, or have they all been local?"

"Actually, our friend Delbert Gingerich came by yesterday. He used to court Elma and lives in LaGrange, although it isn't that far from here."

"Dell's been coming to Topeka to do some work for Elma. And he's been over here to our place for a few barbecues," Joseph added.

Thelma thought about Delbert, and once more, she wondered if there was a chance he and Elma might get together. Delbert had dropped by last night to see the babies and visit with Joseph, but it was after Elma had gone home. If Elma had witnessed Delbert holding little Charles, she may have seen him in a different light. Thelma was almost certain she'd seen a look of longing on his face. Even if he and Elma didn't get together, Thelma hoped Delbert would find a good wife and start a family of his own. Maybe if things worked out like she hoped, his role as a husband and father would be with Elma.

⁓

Elma watched while her parents fussed and cooed over the babies, as Thelma and Joseph stole glances at each other with pure love in their eyes. All their faces beamed, and Elma felt nothing but happiness here in her sister's living room.

Baby Charles and Miriam were her parents' first grandchildren. Elma wondered if she would ever be able to give them more. She'd never been the jealous type, but oh, how it hurt not to be in Thelma's shoes right now as a new mother. If Elma had a husband, at least children could be in her future.

Does Thelma realize the sacrifice I've made giving up my relationship with Ben? Maybe I should confide in her and explain how much Ben means to me. After all, didn't I take a chance that Thelma might move away when I told her she and Joseph belonged together?

Elma forced a smile, which really wasn't hard to do when her father stood and put the baby boy in her arms. She placed her little finger in the infant's grasp, amazed at how tiny his hand was. Her heart melted when Charles yawned and clutched her finger tighter before he fell asleep. All she could do was pray once more, that someday her own baby would be cooing and gripping her finger.

CHAPTER 24

Elma stepped into the phone shack and called Ben. Fully expecting his answering machine to pick up, she was surprised when he answered the phone.

"Hello, Ben, this is Elma." Her fingers grew moist with perspiration, and she wiped them across her brows. "I–I didn't expect you to pick up." Just hearing his voice caused her to stammer.

He chuckled. "You caught me a few minutes after I entered my phone shack to check for messages. It's good to hear from you, Elma. How have you been?"

"I'm fine, and I apologize for not responding to any of your messages." She shifted on her seat. "There's been a lot going on in my life these past weeks, and I've been extra busy."

"What's going on?"

"In addition to running the store, my sister gave birth to twins a week ago. She had a boy and a girl."

"Wow, that's really something! Is everyone doing well?"

"Jah, Thelma and the bopplin are fine. And Joseph. . ." Elma paused to swallow. "Well, he hasn't stopped smiling since they were born."

"No wonder you've been busy. I bet you go over to your sister's place whenever you're not working at the store to help out."

"I did at first, but now my mamm and daed are here, so Mom's taking charge of things. Dad will be heading back to Illinois tomorrow to make sure things are running smoothly at his and Mom's general store, but Mom plans to stay a few more weeks."

Ben didn't say anything for several seconds. Then he cleared his throat loudly. "I'd like to see you again, Elma. Maybe you could come to Grabill on your next day off and stay for supper. I'm sure my mamm would like to show off her new puppy, too."

Elma pinched the bridge of her nose, squeezing her eyes shut. "That sounds nice, but—"

"I won't take no for an answer. I know you're busy, but since your mamm is there to help Thelma, and you've been working hard at the store, you deserve some time off. Don't you agree?"

Elma's tongue darted out to lick her lips. *Would it hurt if I went to Grabill and had supper with Ben and his mother? I should be able to see him once in a while without letting our relationship become serious.*

"Jah, visiting your place would be nice." Elma paused a second. Her throat felt so dry she could barely swallow. "My next day off is this coming Saturday. I'm having some work done inside the store, so it will be closed that day. Would that work for you?"

"Saturday's good. I'll have my driver bring me to your place around three. Maybe we can stop at your sister's before we head for Grabill. I'd like to see the twins and offer congratulations."

Hearing Ben's excited tone caused Elma to wonder if she'd done the right thing accepting his invitation. Going to his house for supper might give the impression she wanted their relationship to become serious. *Which I do,* Elma admitted to herself. *If only I could.*

$\backsim$

When Delbert entered Elma and Thelma's store, he found Lizzie sitting on a stool behind the counter, reading a book. "Where's Elma?" he asked. "She told me she wanted some new shelves built. Since I'll be installing them this Saturday, I came by to see what size she wants."

Without looking up from her book, Lizzie popped a piece of caramel candy into her mouth and chewed on it for what seemed like forever. "Elma's not here right now," she mumbled.

Delbert frowned. Couldn't Lizzie even put the book down and look at him when she spoke? To add to his annoyance, she didn't offer him any candy, even though several pieces lay on the counter. Jelly beans were Delbert's favorite, but he would never pass up a good caramel, either. Some people could be so rude. He'd never understood why Elma hired the woman. In all the times he'd been here, he'd never seen Lizzie doing much except gabbing with the customers.

With mounting irritation, Delbert tapped the toe of his boot against the wooden floor. "Where'd Elma go, and when's she coming back?"

"She ran out to the phone shack to make a few calls and check for messages, so it could be a while."

Still no eye contact from Dizzy Lizzie. It might be wrong to think of her that way, but from all the things Delbert had heard and seen about Elma's helper, it seemed like a fitting name. Of course, he would never call Lizzie "Dizzy" to her face.

The door opened, and Delbert looked in that direction, hoping it was Elma. Instead, two Amish women he'd never met entered the store. He glanced back at Lizzie to see what she would do and was surprised when she set her book aside and greeted the women. *Sure didn't do that when I came in.*

Delbert moved toward the front of the store, where the men's straw hats were sold. He picked one up and looked it over. All his hats were in fairly good condition, so he didn't need a new one, but at least it gave him something to do while he waited for Elma.

He didn't have to wait long, for a few seconds later the door opened again, and she stepped in.

Elma looked in his direction. "Oh hello, Delbert. I wasn't expecting you until Saturday."

He couldn't help noticing her flushed cheeks. "Came by to get the measurements for the shelves you want me to put up."

She lifted both hands and touched her face. "Of course. How silly of me. You'll need to know that before you can do the work. Oh, and when you arrive on Saturday, I'll probably be here long enough to let you in, but the store will be closed the rest of the day."

Blinking rapidly, Delbert crossed his arms. "Isn't it normally open all day on Saturdays?"

She nodded. "Since you'll be working on the new shelves, I

thought it would be best to close the store."

"But you'll still be here, watching me do the task, right?" Almost every time Delbert had done work for Elma, here or at her house, she'd been there, often giving suggestions as to how he should or shouldn't do certain things.

"No, I won't be here in the afternoon."

"Where are you going?"

"To Grabill."

His brows drew together. "What's in Grabill?"

Elma glanced at the counter where Lizzie sat then looked back at Delbert. "I'm going to Grabill with a friend. He wants me to see where he lives."

Delbert tipped his head. "Are you and this fellow courting? Is that what you're saying?"

Elma's gaze dropped to the floor. "Well, sort of."

"How can you sort of be courting? You either are, or you're not." Delbert was sure if Elma was being courted by someone, Joseph would have known about it. And if his friend knew, why hadn't he mentioned it?

"Well, actually, Ben and I have been courting for the past couple of months." Elma spoke in a near whisper.

Delbert's toes curled inside his boots as he bit the inside of his cheek. "Oh, I see. Well, this is the first I've heard of it, but I hope it all works out." Delbert was tempted to say more on the subject but thought better of it. His one big concern was if things got serious between Elma and her suitor who lived in Grabill, would she end up moving there?

∽

Grabill

When Ben hung up the phone, he sat for several minutes, grinning and tapping his fingers on his leg. He felt like singing or shouting. Not only would Elma get to see where he lived, but it was an opportunity for her to become acquainted with his mother.

He held his arms out wide, feeling as though he could hug the whole world. *It's too soon yet, but when the time is right, I'm going to ask*

Elma to marry me.

As the realization hit that he'd invited Elma for supper and hadn't asked Mom, Ben jumped out of his chair. *I'd better get up to the house and make the announcement.*

Ben's long strides took him quickly up the path. Midway, he stopped long enough to jump and click his heels together. Then, taking the porch steps two at a time, he stepped into the house. He found Mom in the kitchen, washing the breakfast dishes.

Mom glanced over her shoulder at Ben while the puppy stood at his feet, barking up at him. "Back already? You weren't at the phone shack very long. Does that mean there were no messages?"

"I don't know. Never checked."

She dropped her sponge into the sink and turned to face him. "How come?"

"When I entered the building, the phone rang, so I answered it." Ben's hands tingled as he spoke rapidly. "Turned out to be Elma, and I. . ." He paused and took a deep breath. "I invited her to come here this Saturday, and she said yes. I'm gonna ask Dave to drive me up to Topeka to get her. Is that okay with you?"

Ben turned his attention to Partner, now tugging on his shoelace. After bending down and scooping the puppy into his arms, Ben ended up with a face full of slurpy kisses. Next, the pup licked his ear.

"Come on now, behave." Ben repositioned the dog in his arms. He hadn't grown much yet and still possessed his milky puppy breath. He couldn't help but like the critter.

Mom's eyebrows furrowed. "Since when do you need my approval to spend time with Elma?"

He scraped a hand through his hair. "Well, the thing is, I invited her for supper. Hope that's okay with you," he added sheepishly.

Mom's shoulders slumped a bit as she slowly nodded. "It's fine. What would you like me to fix?"

"I don't know. Guess you can make anything you want. I don't think Elma's fussy."

"Okay, I'm sure I can come up with something." Mom turned back to the sink and continued to wash the dishes.

Ben looked down at Partner, who had gone limp in his arms and was now asleep. Slowly, he stroked the puppy's head, hoping it would ease this awkward moment. When Mom grew quiet, he knew it best not to say anything more. Ben had a feeling his mother wasn't happy about Elma coming. But once Mom had a chance to spend time with Elma, he felt certain she'd give her blessing.

⁓

Dorothy had been hoping her son had lost interest in the young woman from Topeka. Some time had passed, and it appeared as if the romance might have died down. Now, out of the blue, Ben had invited Elma here for supper. She couldn't help feeling concerned.

Dorothy scrubbed a skillet that didn't want to come clean. She paused to let her hands go limp in the warm water and tried to relax. *I wonder what I should make for Saturday's supper. Ben likes roasted chicken with mashed potatoes. I wonder what Elma likes.*

She grabbed the sponge to wash the next dish. *Ben might be fascinated with Elma, but I still think Martha Graber would have been a better choice for him.*

"Mom, you'd better be careful where you leave things lay." Ben walked up to her, holding the pup. "I found Partner with your slipper in his mouth." He held up her fuzzy blue house shoe.

Dorothy rolled her eyes. "Guess I need to give him some of those chew sticks. He's like a baby, needing to teeth on something for his hurting gums." She chuckled.

"I'm glad you think he's cute." Ben frowned. "Where do you want this wet thing?"

"Put it in my bedroom closet." Dorothy moved from the sink and dried her hands.

"Okay." Ben set the pup on the floor and left the room.

Dorothy's thoughts returned to Elma. The least she could do was give the young woman a chance.

CHAPTER 25

Do you have a problem with your leg?"

Ben jerked his head to look at his driver. "Uh, no. Why do you ask, Dave?" Ever since they'd left Grabill, Ben had been in deep thought, thinking about Elma.

Dave let go of the steering wheel with one hand and pointed. "You've been bouncing that leg for the last ten miles. Are ya nervous about seeing your girl again?"

Ben placed both hands on his knee to keep it from jiggling. "Um, no, not really. Well, maybe a little. This'll be the first time Elma's been to Grabill, and I'm worried she might not like it."

"What's not to like? If you ask me, our little town's a great place to live."

Ben gave a nod. "True, but not everyone likes small towns."

"Topeka's not that big, either."

"Right, but it's close to Shipshewana and several other communities. There's a lot more Amish living in Elma's area, too."

"Are you sure that's all you're worried about—the size of the town and how many Amish live there?" Dave glanced at Ben with brows drawn together; then he looked back at the road again.

Ben swallowed hard while loosening the collar of his shirt. Truth was, he was worried if he and Elma got married that she'd be unwilling to leave her twin sister. But he saw no reason to share that with Dave. Instead, he glanced out his side window and commented on the herd of goats they'd just passed.

Dave gave a little grunt. His cell phone rang then, but like other times, he let it go. He'd once told Ben he didn't like being distracted while he was driving. Besides, it wasn't safe to drive while talking on the phone. Ben couldn't count all the times he'd seen other drivers with their cell phones up to their ears. It seemed to be the thing to do these days.

Ben leaned his head back, closed his eyes, and tried to relax. They'd be in Topeka soon, and he'd feel better once he saw Elma.

⌒

Topeka

Needing something to do with her hands, Elma nibbled on a handful of almonds, which probably was a mistake, because now she'd need to brush her teeth again before Ben arrived.

She glanced at her cat as he lay purring under the dining-room table.

"Wish I felt as relaxed as you look," Elma murmured before heading to the bathroom.

After brushing her teeth, she stared at her reflection in the mirror. *Kapp on straight, no cat hairs showing.* Satisfied with her appearance, she went to get her handbag. A quick glance at the clock, and she hurried out the door. The butterflies in her stomach were hard at work as she took a seat on the porch.

While Elma waited nervously for Ben's arrival, she made a mental list of everything she had done to be sure she hadn't forgotten anything. She'd put the dog in the basement a while ago and then gone out to the store to check on Delbert. He was doing fine on his own and seemed a bit perturbed when she'd come in asking questions. *But that's just Delbert. He never has liked it when he's doing a job for me and I check on him or offer suggestions.*

Elma stepped off the porch and strolled around her vegetable garden. Some potatoes, carrots, and beets remained to be dug up, but other than those areas, the garden was bare. It was just as well. She didn't have time to do much in the way of preserving right now. Dad had gone home to Illinois, and Mom would follow within the next few weeks; then Elma would need to help Thelma as often as she could, with little time for other things. So it was good she was seeing

Ben this evening, because after tonight she might not have time for much socializing.

Elma's attention turned to the road when she heard a vehicle approach. Her heartbeat quickened as a van pulled in and she saw Ben inside with his driver, Dave. Elma rushed out to meet them, eager to take Ben across the street to meet her niece and nephew.

⟳

Although not quite finished with his job, Delbert set his tools aside and went to the front of the store to sit on the stool behind the counter and eat the candy bar he'd brought along. After finishing the treat, he ambled over to the window and looked out. Delbert watched with interest as a van pulled into Elma's yard. A few seconds later, an Amish man got out. They stood beside each other for a bit then got into the van. The vehicle pulled across the street and up Thelma and Joe's driveway. Elma and the Amish man got out and went inside.

Delbert pressed his nose against the window. *I bet that's the man who's been courting her.* Delbert needed to get back to work, but he couldn't keep from watching. His lips grew tight as he thought about the days he'd courted Elma. Truth was, they'd never had much to say to each other unless she was scolding or questioning him about something, and he was constantly defending himself.

Delbert wondered what would have happened if he hadn't stopped courting Elma. He slapped the side of his head. *Why am I even thinking such thoughts when Elma always got under my skin and annoyed me to no end?*

Seeing Elma with another man was like watching a possibility fade away. For some reason his heart did a flip-flop and sadness quickly took over.

⟳

Thelma had finished feeding and diapering the babies when a knock sounded on the door.

"I'll get it." Mom rose from the rocking chair, where she'd sat burping Miriam a few minutes ago. She hurried from the nursery.

Thelma was about to put the babies in their bassinets when

Mom returned, saying Elma was here, along with an Amish man who'd introduced himself as Benjamin Wagler. "They're on their way to Grabill and said they stopped by here first to see the bopplin," she added.

Thelma frowned, brushing some baby powder off her blue dress. "I can't believe Elma agreed to go there with Ben. I told her we planned to have Delbert over this evening to finally eat those fish he and Joseph caught a few weeks ago."

Mom tipped her head. "Are you still trying to get those two together?"

"I'm not pushing things, but it would be nice if it happened." Thelma handed Charles to her mother then picked up Miriam.

Mom tapped her shoulder. "You know the old saying, 'Love has no bounds.' If your sister chooses that young man in the other room, you won't have an easy time changing her mind."

Thelma's shoulders slumped as she lowered her voice. "To tell you the truth, I'm struggling with the issue. Why can't she be content with Delbert?"

"It's not up to you to choose for her. Please think about it, and a little praying would also help. Besides, Elma didn't decide Joseph was the one for you. You did."

"You're right. Guess we'd better go out and say hello."

Upon entering the living room, Thelma's heart clenched when she saw Elma and Ben sitting on the couch, wearing big smiles as they engaged in conversation. In all the time Delbert and Elma had been courting, she'd never seen her sister look so happy and relaxed.

That's how it's always been with me and Joseph. Thelma moved toward the couch. "It's nice to see you, Ben. I understand you came by to see our twins."

His eyes brightened as he bobbed his head. "I expected to see their daed here, too."

"Joseph will be home later. He had some work to get done at the harness shop today." Thelma handed Miriam to Elma then looked at Ben. "Would you like to hold our little Charlie, or do bopplin make you naerfich?"

"I'm not nervous at all." He held out his arms. "I would very much like to hold him."

Thelma put the baby in Ben's arms and was surprised to see how at ease he seemed to be as he placed Charles against his shoulder and patted the baby's back. It seemed strange that a man who had no children would appear so relaxed. Even Joseph acted nervous when he first held the twins.

"You've been blessed with two fine-looking bopplin." Ben chuckled when little Charlie let out a healthy burp. "And this one's already learning what it is to be a man."

"Miriam can burp pretty loud, too," Elma interjected. "I've heard her on several occasions."

"It's amazing how small we start off when we enter the world." Ben stared at the babies.

"Jah. These little ones have a ways to go, but they will grow too quickly, I'm afraid," Mom responded.

Thelma and Mom both took seats in the chairs opposite the couch, and everyone visited awhile, with the conversation revolving mostly around the babies.

When a horn tooted outside, Ben stood and handed Charles back to Thelma. "I think my driver is getting anxious to go."

"You could invite him in," Mom suggested.

Ben shook his head. "Elma and I need to get going anyway. I want Dave to drive us around Grabill before it gets dark so Elma can see what she thinks of the area."

Elma stood, too, and gave Miriam to Mom. Then she turned to face Thelma. "I don't know how late I'll be, so when Delbert finishes at the store, would you ask Joseph to go over and make sure all the doors are locked?"

"Of course. But since Delbert will be joining us for supper, we can ask if he locked up."

A rosy color erupted on Elma's cheeks. "Oh, that's right, I'd forgotten he was coming here for the evening meal."

Thelma's forehead wrinkled. *How could my sister have forgotten? It was only a few days ago when I mentioned our plans and invited her to join us for the fish fry.* Thelma determined that apparently the only thing on Elma's mind right now was spending time with Ben. Her concern over losing her sister grew as she said good-bye to Ben and Elma and watched them head outside, both all smiles. If this relationship wasn't nipped soon, she might lose her sister to Ben Wagler, as well as to the town of Grabill.

Chapter 26

Grabill

As Dave drove Ben and Elma around Grabill, Ben pointed out the various sights. They went past an Amish-run fabric store, two grocery stores—one owned by the Amish and one by the English. They also saw a feed store, buggy shop, health food store, machine shop, the local library, and two Amish schools. As they passed several buggies on the road, Ben explained that the Grabill Amish only drove open buggies.

"How interesting. I bet it can get a bit chilly in the winter," she responded.

"Jah, but we manage."

"That's Miller's Country Store over there," Dave put in. "They sell everything from housewares, shoes, sewing notions, china dishes, baby things, and vitamins." He glanced over his shoulder at Elma. "They even carry stoves and refrigerators."

Elma sucked in her breath. The exterior of the building made her and Thelma's store look small by comparison. She'd have to hire a lot more help if she and her sister owned such a big place.

"There's Nolt's Dinner House, where a lot of English folks like to go for a taste of Amish-style cooking," Ben commented as Dave turned his van onto another road. "My mom's and my place will be coming up soon."

Elma's hands grew sweaty as she clasped them tightly in her lap. *I hope this evening goes well. What if his mother doesn't like me?*

"So what do you think of Grabill?" Ben's elbow connected gently with Elma's arm. "Do you think you could ever live here?"

Unsure of how to respond, she smiled and said, "It's a lovely town—although smaller than Topeka or Shipshewana."

"But that's the beauty of it," Dave interjected. "Fewer tourists come here."

"And we can go about our lives without so many curious stares from outsiders. Not all English are like Dave," Ben was quick to say.

When he paused, Elma felt him watching her. She turned toward him, unable to look away.

"So could you ever live here?" Ben asked again.

She dropped her gaze. "I don't think so. Thelma needs me in Topeka, not to mention I have a business to run. . . . What about you?" she dared to ask. "Could you move from Grabill and start over someplace else?"

"It would be hard for me to leave." Rubbing his hand against the front of his shirt, Ben's lips pressed together in a slight grimace. "Grabill's my home, and I have a responsibility to take care of my mamm, as well as my horseshoeing business."

Elma's chest tightened. *Then why are we carrying on this long-distance relationship that can go nowhere?* She clasped her fingers tightly around her purse straps. *I should never have agreed to come here today. But, oh, I do enjoy being with you, Ben. If only you lived in Topeka, or could move there to be closer to me.*

⁓

Dorothy opened the oven door to check on the roast. It poked tender, so she turned the temperature to low. After closing the oven door, she looked up at the clock above the refrigerator. Ben and his guest should be here soon, so she might as well put the potatoes on to boil. If they got done before Ben and Elma arrived, she would put the kettle on a low burner to keep them warm.

Dorothy put the fruit salad she'd made in the refrigerator and began setting the table. After placing silverware beside each plate, she heard the back door creak open and click shut. A few seconds later, Ben stepped into the room with a lovely young Amish woman at his side.

"Mom, I'd like you to meet Elma Hochstetler."

"Jah, we've met. When I went into her store once, with my friend Eileen. I'm sure I mentioned it to you, Ben." Dorothy gave Elma a hug, as she didn't want to appear unwelcoming. "It's nice to see you again."

Elma nodded. "It's nice to see you, too. I didn't realize when we met that you were Ben's mamm, however. What a coincidence."

"Maybe it wasn't." Ben looked over at Elma and grinned. "It could have been fate—like the day the two of us met at the farmers' market in Shipshe."

Ben's beaming expression and glowing cheeks said it all—he was in love with Elma.

⌒⌒

"Is there anything I can do to help with supper?" Elma asked, setting her purse on the floor in the corner of the room.

Mom was about to respond when Partner bounded into the kitchen, yipping up a storm.

Elma raised a hand to her mouth, giggling as the puppy slid to a stop at Ben's feet.

"Hey little fellow, did ya miss me today?" Ben squatted down to greet the small dog.

Elma went on her knees beside him. "What a *lieblich* pup." Partner licked her hand when she reached out to stroke his ears.

Ben looked up at Mom in time to see her wrinkle her nose. "Oh, he's adorable all right, but not when he's stirring up mischief. He got into my knitting basket earlier and unraveled a ball of yarn. Why, the little schtinker even pulled one of Ben's *hemmer* out of the laundry basket this morning and dragged it all over the yard. I had quite the time chasing after him."

Ben chuckled. "I'll bet it was a sight to behold."

She shook her finger. "It's not funny, and you're fortunate the shirt didn't end up with more than a little dirt on it. Partner could have put a hole in the sleeve."

"Partner?" Elma tipped her head. "Is that the puppy's name?"

Ben gave a nod. "Haven't had him very long. Mom brought the pup home after my dog, Hunter, disappeared." He gave Partner a pat

171

on the head. "It'll be a while before he's old enough to do any bird hunting, but I hope to begin early training for him later this fall. Hunter could work a field real good when he was hunting birds. I'm hoping Partner will take after him in that regard."

Elma lifted Partner's chin and gazed at him. "It's amazing how much he looks like my dog, Freckles." She shrugged her shoulders. "But then I suppose most German shorthairs look similar."

"Jah." Ben rose to his full height, and Elma stood, too. "Well, now that we've both got our hands all doggied, guess we'd better wash up or Mom won't let us sit down at her supper table. You can go first, Elma."

She took a few steps forward but hesitated, looking quizzically at Ben.

"The bathroom's down the hall—second door on the right." Mom pointed in that direction.

"Okay, danki." A deep flush crept across Elma's cheeks as she hurried from the room.

᛫

A short time later, they all went to the dining room. Ben's mother directed Elma to have a seat next to Ben. The table was set with pretty pink-and-white floral china and a cream-colored tablecloth. Dorothy had obviously put some thought into this visit.

They prayed silently, and then Dorothy passed the roast and potatoes. They also circulated a mixed green salad, steamed carrots, and broccoli.

"This is a tender roast, Mom. Very good." Ben smiled in her direction.

Elma nodded in agreement.

"Your daed taught me how to pick the choicest cuts of meat." Dorothy looked across the table at Elma. "This is one of Ben's favorite meals."

"I can understand why." Elma ate some potatoes. "Everything is delicious." *Ben's mamm is a good cook, and she knows how to do up a fancy table.*

"I made a blueberry and a cherry pie for dessert." Dorothy took a drink of water.

Ben scooted his chair in closer. "Wait till you taste my mamm's pies. She's the best baker."

"It sounds tempting. I hope I'll have room for it after all this supper."

Dorothy gave a quick wave of her hand. "Well, if you don't, I'll send some home with you."

Elma smiled. "Danki."

"Mom's also quite the yodeler."

"Is that so?" Elma's ears perked up. "I've always admired people who could yodel."

"It's part of Swiss Amish heritage here in Grabill. Maybe she'll sing and yodel for us after supper." Ben looked at his mother with expectancy.

"We'll see about that." Her cheeks colored. "I understand Ben showed you around our small town. What did you think of Grabill, Elma?"

"It's a nice place. There seems to be plenty of shops, plus a few restaurants." Elma took a bite of mashed potatoes.

"At times I go with my friends to one of the larger towns. The variety we get here can't match those of the larger stores."

Ben picked up a pretty etched-glass dish and spooned some of its contents onto his plate. "My mamm makes some good apple butter. If you have room, give it a try on a piece of bread." He placed the small jar near Elma.

Elma scooped a spoonful and put it near her salad. She ate some mixed with the lettuce. "This is good."

Dorothy beamed then changed the conversation back to shopping.

⟳

Elma remained quiet during most of the drive home. She'd enjoyed spending time with Ben this evening and getting to know his mother. The meal had been good, and after Dorothy sang and yodeled a few songs, they'd had fun eating popcorn while working on a puzzle for a short time. Partner had taken a liking to her and had even fallen asleep in her lap. She meshed okay with Dorothy, too, although Ben's mother seemed a bit reserved when they talked. Deep down, Elma's feelings were growing for Ben, but she couldn't stop thinking about what he'd told her earlier—that his home was in Grabill and he bore responsibility for his mom. Ben obviously had no plans to move.

Well, neither do I. She folded her arms, staring out the van window into the darkened sky. *So where does that leave us? Certainly not with a future together.*

Elma felt the warmth of his skin as he took hold of her hand. She felt certain he cared for her. But was it enough to leave Grabill and move to Topeka? Ben hadn't said anything about marriage, so it would be improper to bring the topic up. But what was the point in continuing to see him when neither of them were willing or able to relocate?

She squeezed her eyes shut. *Should I tell him when he walks me to my door that I don't think we should see each other anymore? I should never have agreed to spend the afternoon and evening with Ben. I let my feelings for him get in the way of good sense, and now saying good-bye will be that much harder.*

Elma's skin tingled as Ben stroked her hand tenderly with his thumb. *I can't tell him tonight. I'll wait a few days, or even a week, and then write Ben a letter, explaining why I can't see him anymore. Surely he'll understand and won't call or come around. It's best for both of us if we don't carry this relationship any further.*

CHAPTER 27

The next Friday evening, after Ben finished working for the day, it was all he could do to put his horse away. Bending over to shoe for a good many hours had caused his back to spasm. "I should go see the local chiropractor," he mumbled. "My back's in bad shape." As much as he enjoyed his line of work, Ben figured he might have to give it up someday. But for now, it helped pay the bills, along with what they got from farming, as well as the sale of Mom's garden produce and flowers.

Gritting his teeth, Ben limped toward the house. All he wanted to do was eat a little something, take a long hot bath, and stretch out on his bed. He didn't have much appetite for food and hoped Mom hadn't cooked a big meal.

Tomorrow, if his back felt better and his driver was available, Ben planned to head up to Topeka to see Elma. Last night he'd called and left a message, saying he hoped to come by on Saturday, and if she was free, he wanted to take her out for supper.

Sure wish Topeka was closer. Ben reached around to rub the sorest spot on his back. *At least I could go with my horse and buggy instead of spending the money to hire Dave or one of our other drivers.*

When Ben reached the back porch, he paused to reflect on the conversation he'd had with Elma last Saturday when they'd been driving around Grabill. She'd made it clear that she had no intention of relocating, and since he didn't plan to move, either, there was no point in continuing to pursue her—unless he could convince Elma to change her mind about moving. And that could only happen if he kept seeing her.

Ben grasped the door handle and stepped inside. He sat on the bench inside the utility room and removed his boots, being careful not to strain his back further.

Still wearing his stockings, Ben made his way to the kitchen.

"Hey, Ben. Supper will be ready soon. Oh, and there's a letter for you from Elma." Mom turned from where she stood at the stove and pointed to the kitchen table. "It came in today's mail."

Eager to see what Elma had written, Ben took a seat and tore the envelope open.

Bending his neck forward, he pressed his hands to his temples as he silently read her message:

Dear Ben:
There's no easy way to say this, but I've come to the conclusion that we should stop seeing each other. Your place is in Grabill with your mother, and mine is here in Topeka, with my twin sister and her family.

You are a kindhearted man, who deserves to be happy, and I wish you all the best in the days to come.

Fondly,
Elma

"Is everything okay?" Mom asked. "You look umgerennt."

At a loss for words, Ben turned away, covering his mouth.

Mom placed a lid on the kettle she'd been stirring and moved over to the table. "Did Elma say something upsetting?" She put both hands on Ben's shoulders.

He swallowed hard. "She doesn't want to see me anymore."

"Really? How come?"

"Elma wants to stay in Topeka, and my place is here, so she's right—there's no point in continuing to see each other, since we have no future together."

Mom massaged his tense shoulders. "Maybe it's for the best, son. A long-distance relationship is difficult, and since neither of you is free to move. . ."

Ben pushed his chair away from the table. "My back hurts, Mom. I'm gonna take a bath and go to bed."

"What about supper?"

"Sorry, but I'm not hungerich. Maybe I can have some of what you made for lunch or supper tomorrow, since I won't be going to Topeka like I'd planned." Holding his back, he bent slightly forward and shuffled out of the room. He needed to be alone to rest and sort things out.

⌒

Topeka

"Are you hungry, boy?" Elma placed a bowl of dog food on the floor next to Freckles' water dish. She'd finished eating supper herself and still needed to do the dishes, but she wanted to get Freckles and Tiger fed first.

Elma still thought it was surprising how Freckles had acted last week after Ben and Dave dropped her off. When she'd taken the dog outside and sat on the porch steps to wait, instead of Freckles going into the yard, he didn't leave her side. He sniffed her from head to toe. At first, she thought it was normal, with the scent from Dorothy's puppy lingering on her clothes. But it wasn't only that—it was how Freckles kept whining that seemed so odd and caused Elma to wonder why it took the dog a while to settle down.

She shook her head. *If only animals could talk.*

While Freckles ate, Elma poured Tiger his food, placing it in the opposite corner of the room. If she didn't keep her pets' dishes separated, they would often try to horn in on each other's food.

Once that chore was done, Elma went to the sink and filled it with warm, soapy water. As she sloshed the sponge over each dirty dish, her thoughts went to Ben. *I wonder if he received my letter yet? If so, what was his reaction?* Her nose and throat burned with unshed tears. *I hope he understands and doesn't try to contact me. If I see him again, it'll only make things harder.*

A few minutes later, Tiger left his dish and came over to sit beside Elma, swishing his fluffy tail against her leg. *Meow! Meow!*

Elma looked down. "Did you come here to offer me comfort, or are you needing some attention?"

The cat looked up at her and purred.

Elma smiled, despite her melancholy mood. "I'll take that as a yes to both."

⁓

"Did you notice how sullen your sister seemed when she was here for supper last night?" Mom commented as she sat beside Thelma on the living-room couch, each of them holding a baby.

Thelma shook her head. "To tell you the truth, I was so busy with the bopplin, I hadn't noticed. Did she say anything was bothering her?"

Mom shook her head. "No. She just wasn't her usual perky self."

"Maybe she was mied. Since I'm not able to help at the store anymore, Elma's been working longer hours, which would make anyone tired." Thelma placed Miriam tummy-down across her lap and patted the infant's back. Sometimes that position worked best to get her to burp. "What my sister needs to do is hire another helper. Lizzie's a nice person, but she can't do many things and tends to talk too much when she should be working." Once Miriam burped, Thelma cradled the baby in her arms. "I'm not saying Elma should let Lizzie go—just hire an additional person."

Mom slowly nodded. "I'd hoped to help out in the store while I was here, but my first priority is to help you with the twins." She patted little Charlie on the back and smiled when he let out a healthy burp.

Tears welled in Thelma's eyes. "Having you here has meant a lot to me. I can't thank you enough."

"It's been my pleasure. I only wish I could stay longer."

Thelma swallowed hard, determined not to give in to her tears. "Dad needs you back home, and when you leave next week, we'll manage on our own, just as you did after Elma and I were born."

Mom's forehead wrinkled. "That was a little different. I had four sisters plus my mamm to help me back then. All you have is Elma, and because of the store, she can't be over here all the time."

"Which is why I am going to ask some of the women in our church district to help out. Several have volunteered already, so it shouldn't be a problem."

Mom reached over and touched Thelma's arm. "Your daed and I will be back for Christmas. Maybe we can stay till New Year's, too."

"That'd be nice. It'll give Elma and me something to look forward to. Hopefully Joseph's parents can be here, too, although they will probably spend part of the holidays with other family members." Thelma sighed. "It's important for family to be together as often as they can."

CHAPTER 28

Grabill

Throughout the holidays Ben moped around, spending much of his free time in his bedroom. He'd gone in for a few chiropractic treatments because of his back. They seemed to help, and he experienced less discomfort while he worked.

As Ben stood in front of his bedroom closet, he thought about his job and wondered what other kind of work he could do. He enjoyed meeting people and keeping informed on things. He also needed a job that would pay a decent wage. Here it was, the first of January already, and a whole new year lay ahead—a year in which he had nothing to look forward to.

It was hard to think about going through the rest of his life without Elma. Even though he'd known her a short time, his heart told him he'd never feel for any other woman what he did for her. But if she wouldn't leave Topeka, being together was out of the question, for Ben couldn't leave his mother in the lurch. In addition to needing to support herself, she'd be lonely living in this big old house alone.

Maybe Mom had been right when she'd said it was better this way. Elma had an obligation to her family, same as him. Truth was, Ben wished he'd never met her at the farmers' market. If he hadn't been looking at the produce on her table and had a little mishap, he wouldn't feel like there was a hole in his heart right now.

Ben stopped pacing to look out his window. He stared at the swirling snow which was quickly covering the ground. It was the first snowfall they'd had this winter, but the beautiful trees in their yard, wearing blankets of white, did nothing to lift his spirits. Back when

Ben was a boy, he loved playing in the snow. Even as a young man, it was fun to romp in the white stuff with his dog.

Ben didn't know how he'd made it through the holidays. All he could think about was the fun he and Elma were missing out on, enjoying the snow together. First Hunter, and now Elma—both of them gone from his life.

"Hunter," Ben murmured, pressing his forehead against the cold window glass. "I hope you found a new master who's been taking good care of you."

While Partner had filled a void in Ben's life, he'd never felt as close to the pup as he had to Hunter. As far as Ben was concerned, the puppy was more Mom's dog than his. But that was okay. She needed the pup's companionship whenever Ben was away.

Compelled to seek God's will for his life, Ben took a seat on the end of his bed, reflecting on Proverbs 16:9, a verse he'd committed to memory some time ago: *"A man's heart deviseth his way: but the LORD directeth his steps."*

He bowed his head. *Heavenly Father, please guide and direct my life in the year ahead, and if Your will is for me to get married, send the right woman into my life who'll be happy living in Grabill, or help me to be content as a bachelor. Amen.*

Topeka

As Elma sat watching her parents hold Miriam and Charles, a deep sadness welled in her soul. In addition to feeling bad because Mom was going home tomorrow, she struggled with envy yet again because she had no children. Mom's nonstop talk about how much the babies had grown and how she was going to miss them when she went home only added to Elma's resentment.

Her parents had experienced the joy of raising twins, and now Thelma and Joseph had been given the same opportunity. Elma didn't even have a husband, much less the prospect of becoming a parent.

She glanced across the room to where Delbert and Joseph sat playing checkers. Elma wondered if Delbert had been invited to join them for a meal and to spend the evening playing games because he was lonely, or if Thelma had planned it to try and get her and Delbert back together. Elma was pretty sure it was the latter, since this wasn't the first time Delbert had been invited to her sister's house when she was there for a meal. Somehow it always worked out so that Elma was seated next to or directly across the table from him.

Delbert's blond hair seemed a bit thinner these days, and Elma noticed he had a patch of eczema on the back of his neck. *Probably from eating too many sugar-laden sweets and unhealthy snacks. He needs a wife to cook him some decent meals.*

"King me! That's it—I won!" Delbert clapped his hands, causing everyone in the room to jump except Elma. Delbert was a sharp cookie when it came to most games, and it didn't surprise her in the least that he'd beaten Joseph at checkers. Delbert always got excited when he won, too.

She glanced at the babies and was surprised they'd both slept through the noise.

"Hey, Elma, why don't ya come over here and see if you can beat me at checkers? As I recall, you're pretty good at this game."

Unable to say no to the challenge, Elma rose from her comfortable chair and took Joseph's seat at the dining-room table. Joseph winked at Elma before settling himself in the love seat beside Thelma.

And who might you be cheering for? she almost asked out loud.

Delbert insisted Elma begin the game, and as things got started, a desire to win crept in. She'd always liked a good challenge, and playing against Delbert was definitely that. Elma had to think fast while calculating each move in order to stay up with him.

When his next turn came, Delbert took some time then slid his game piece.

Elma studied the board, wondering why he'd moved it there. She made her next move and took another one of his checkers. "Your turn, Delbert."

He squinted, looking at her suspiciously. "Again? How are you doing that?"

She smiled, feeling a bit smug. "I know how to play this game, and you seem to be losing your edge."

"I'm doing fine. I only slipped up a little," Delbert mumbled.

Halfway through the game, Thelma and Joseph left the room to make popcorn.

Despite the challenge of trying to outsmart Delbert, for the first time all day, Elma was enjoying herself. The icing on the cake, so to speak, was that for the first time in many weeks, Ben Wagler was not at the center of her thoughts.

⌒ᗧ

Thelma smiled at Joseph as he got out the popcorn maker and placed it on the stove. She felt grateful to have a husband who enjoyed being with her and was willing to help. She chuckled to herself. *Of course, his enjoyment of popcorn might have something to do with his eagerness to make it.*

She handed him the container of coconut oil—a Christmas gift from Elma. Her sister might have thought she was being subtle, but Thelma knew the reason for this particular gift was to make sure she was cooking with a healthy oil. As always, Thelma's twin was looking out for her welfare.

While Joseph took care of the popcorn, Thelma brewed a pot of coffee and sliced some pumpkin bread Mom had made yesterday. What a joy it had been to have her mother with them from Christmas to New Year's. Thelma looked forward to spring, when she and Joseph hoped to take their little ones on their first trip to see their grandparents in Sullivan, Illinois. It would also be nice to introduce Miriam and Charles to all the aunts, uncles, and cousins she and Elma had grown up with.

After all the doting and holding our twins will get, they'll be spoiled by the time we come home, she mused.

When the corn was done popping and Thelma had a tray filled with pumpkin bread ready, she took cups and small plates down from the cupboard.

"If you want to carry the popcorn and bread to the dining-room table, I'll bring the coffeepot, plates, and silverware," Joseph offered. "Oh, and some napkins, too."

She nodded. "I'll do that in a minute, but first I'd like to ask you something."

He turned to face her. "What is it, my dear fraa?"

Thelma smiled at his endearing words. "It's about Delbert."

"You think he's taken all of Elma's checker pieces by now?"

"Probably, but that's not what I was going to ask." She moved closer to him and spoke in a low tone. "Do you think Delbert might still be interested in my sister?"

His eyes widened. "Now what would make you ask such a question?"

She lifted her shoulders. "Oh, I don't know. Maybe it's wishful thinking on my part, but it does seem like he and Elma are getting along better these days. Remember how she laughed at all his jokes when he stopped by on Christmas Eve?"

"Jah, but then we all were laughing." Joseph placed both hands on Thelma's shoulders. "I wouldn't make too much of it if I were you."

"Oh, I'm not. I just think. . ."

Joseph bent his head and kissed the end of her nose. "If Dell and Elma are meant to be together, it'll happen without any help from either of us. Now let's get back there and watch those two play the rest of the game. I'm sure if one of 'em had won, we'd have heard a bit of commotion by now."

Thelma snickered. "You're right about that." She picked up the bowl of popcorn and tray full of pumpkin bread and entered the dining room in time to hear Elma shout, "King me, Delbert! End of game!"

CHAPTER 29

By the middle of March, Thelma had settled into a routine with the twins. It was hard to believe they were five and a half months old already. Time seemed to be slipping by so quickly.

Thelma sat in the rocker, mending a pair of Joseph's trousers, but glanced up every once in a while to check on the babies. They were both wide awake, rolling and scooching around in their playpen, while making all sorts of unintelligible baby noises.

She chuckled when little Charlie reached for a rattle and Miriam grabbed ahold of it first. It looked like a bit of sibling rivalry had already begun. No doubt, it would get worse as they grew. Of course, she and Joseph, as any good parents, would teach the twins to share and try to work out their problems.

Thelma reflected on her and Elma's childhood. For the most part, they'd gotten along well, and being identical twins, they usually were treated the same. However, Thelma recalled how one time, when she'd gone shopping with Dad, he'd bought her an ice-cream cone. After returning home, she'd mentioned getting the treat, and Elma became upset. There'd also been a little rivalry whenever Thelma and Elma played games. Most times, though, Thelma let her sister win in order to keep the peace.

She glanced at her babies again and smiled. They'd both fallen asleep, only now Charlie held the favorite rattle. As the children grew, it would be interesting to see who would become the more dominant twin.

A clap of thunder in the distance drove Thelma's thoughts aside.

The howling wind and patter of rain hitting the window indicated a storm was brewing. As the skies darkened, so did the inside of the house. Thelma got up and lit the gas lamp hanging overhead. She went to the kitchen and lit that one, too. Dinner cooked in the oven, and the smell of roasting chicken made her mouth water. The warm glow emanating from the lamp felt soothing.

Thelma got out some carrots and cucumbers to go with the meal. Once she'd finished cutting the veggies, she returned to the other room to check on her little ones. They were both still sleeping, so she quietly took a seat in her rocker.

After mending Joseph's pants, she reached for one of her knitting projects. She'd started a peach-colored pot holder the other day and couldn't wait to finish it.

Thelma looked up at the clock on the fireplace mantel. Joseph would be getting off work soon. She hoped the rain would let up before he headed home. Well, at least he'd be driving his closed-in buggy this evening. It was never fun to ride in an open buggy and get caught in the rain. She wondered how the Amish who lived in Grabill managed in their open buggies during rainy and snowy weather.

Thoughts of Grabill made Thelma think about Elma and how she'd told her that she had broken things off with Ben Wagler. In the long run, it was for the best, since they lived so far from each other. Still, it distressed Thelma to see her sister unhappy. But these last few months, Elma seemed more relaxed. Maybe the pain of breaking up with Ben had eased.

⁓

"How's it going today, Lizzie?" Delbert asked as he entered the store and crossed over to the counter where the older woman sat working on a crossword puzzle. At least this time she wasn't reading a book or munching on candy—although he couldn't figure out why she was sitting here at all, since there were no customers to wait on at the moment. Shouldn't she be stocking shelves or something?

Lizzie looked at him and blinked several times. "Well, Delbert. I didn't realize you'd come into the store."

"Just got here, and I asked you a question." He folded his arms.

"Apparently you didn't hear me, though."

Her cheeks reddened, and she set the crossword puzzle aside. "Sorry about that. Guess I was a little preoccupied."

His eyebrows pinched together. *What else is new?*

"What was your question?"

"I asked how it's going."

She smiled. "Everything's fine and dandy here. Oh, and if you're looking for Elma, she's in the back room." Lizzie motioned in that direction with her head.

"I'll head back there now." Delbert paused and tapped the countertop lightly with the palm of his hand. "Don't work too hard, Lizzie."

Before she could comment, he scurried down the nearest aisle. He was at the door of the back room when Elma stepped out, nearly colliding with him.

"Ach, I didn't know you were there." A flush of pink crept across her cheeks as he clasped her arms to keep them from bumping into each other.

"Sorry about that. Are you okay?"

"Jah. You just surprised me, is all."

He wiggled his brows. "That's me—always full of surprises."

She smiled. "I assume you're on your way home from somewhere. Did you stop by the store for a reason or to get out of the rain till it passes?"

"The rain doesn't bother me, but I have another reason for stopping. I'm hungerich and don't want to wait till I get back to LaGrange to eat supper." He released his hold on her arms and took a step back. "I was wondering if you'd like to go out to supper with me. We can either go to Tiffany's or one of the Mexican restaurants in town."

She looked down, then back up at him again while shuffling her feet. "I don't have anything definite planned for supper, so jah, I'd be happy to accept your invitation. But what about the nasty weather we're having?"

Delbert grinned. "Don't worry about that. See. . ." He pointed toward the window. "It's a steady rain now and not blowing like it was before. I'll hang around here till you're ready to close the store. Then we can head to the restaurant of your choice. Oh, and you might want to bring an umbrella with you."

"I'll need to let Freckles outside for a while before we go. He's been in the basement most of the day, except when I went home for a short time around noon. I'm sure the thunder has him worked up by now, too."

"No problem. I can wait. You know what, though, Elma?"

"What?"

"You oughta let me build a doghouse and a chain-link fence around it so the dog can be outside during the day when you're not home. It's not good for a hund—especially one his size—to be cooped up in the basement for hours on end."

Elma nodded. "You're right. I'd thought about asking but wasn't sure if you'd have the time."

"Even if I didn't, I would make the time." He brushed his hand lightly over her arm. "That's what friends are for." Truth was, Delbert had come to see Elma as a good friend.

⌒

"Sure am glad the rain's stopped. It was comin' down pretty hard for a while there," Delbert commented as he and Elma entered El Zorrito's Mexican Restaurant.

Elma nodded, holding her wet umbrella away from her dress. "The sky still looks a bit ominous."

He tipped his head. "Ominous?"

"Jah—threatening."

"Oh, you mean the dark, low-hanging clouds that seem to be moving toward LaGrange?"

"Right. Sure hope we don't get a really bad storm—or worse yet a tornado."

"It's been some time since one touched down around these parts." Delbert led Elma to a table near the window. "Think the last tornado I heard about here in Indiana happened in Kokomo. There was a bad one in Nappanee several years ago, too. Many of us Amish in the area went there afterward to help repair the damage. That was before you and Thelma moved here, though."

Leaning toward the window, Elma shivered as she took another look at the sky. She bit her lips when she noticed, off in the distance, how its color had changed to a sickly green. The air had felt strange when they'd gotten out of the buggy and walked through the parking lot—like a quiet calm settling over the area. The eerie silence had been unnerving, as though a prelude of something about to happen.

Elma glanced toward one of the trees near the hitching rail where Delbert's buggy was parked. Not a single branch moved. Nothing in the air was stirring, not even a bird. Although a few tornadoes had touched down in her home state of Illinois, including Sullivan, none had ever hit her parents' home, for which she felt grateful.

Another shiver went up Elma's spine as she forced herself to look away.

Delbert reached across the table and patted her outstretched hand. "Don't look so worried. I'm sure we'll be fine. Just remember, as long as we don't hear about any tornado warnings or sirens, there's nothing to worry about." He picked up his menu. "Now let's try to relax and enjoy the evening. Think I'll have the arroz con pollo. What sounds good to you?"

"I might have the chicken fajitas." Thinking about how good this restaurant's food was made Elma's mouth water. Even the chips they served were good, although the salsa was a bit too hot for her liking.

Her mind went back to an evening a few years ago when she, Thelma, Joseph, and Delbert had shared pizza together. Delbert had added hot sauce to his, and Elma foolishly tried some. She'd never forget the burning sensation. It felt like her whole mouth was on fire.

When a waiter came to take their orders, Elma asked for a side order of mild salsa to go with the chips he'd placed on the table. The lights flickered overhead, and a murmur went through the restaurant.

"Sure hope we don't lose power." Their dark-haired waiter frowned. "We don't have a generator, so when the power goes out we can't cook. Hopefully it won't happen tonight." He turned to put in their orders and returned a few minutes later with their beverages.

There weren't any more disturbances with the lights, and everything seemed to be fine. Elma and Delbert bowed their heads for silent prayer, and then, while they munched on the chips, Delbert brought up the topic of Elma's dog again.

"Sure am glad you were willing to take Freckles. When he showed up at my house, I didn't know what to do with him."

She leaned both elbows on the table, gazing across at him. "I'm curious about something, Delbert."

"What's that?"

"You seem to like the dog. How come you didn't want to keep him?"

He shifted in his chair, looking down at the table. "Other than Joe, I've never told anyone this before, but I used to have a good hunting dog when I was a teenager." His voice faltered. "After she got hit by a car and died in my arms, I swore I'd never own another hund. *Es hot arig wehgeduh*, and I never want to get attached to another pet and put myself through something like that."

Her heart went out to him. "I understand that it was very painful. Loss is always hard, but life goes on. As Christians, we need to enjoy each new day and thank the Lord for all He's given us."

"I do thank Him. Just don't want to put myself in the position to lose another hund."

Elma was about to respond when their waiter, wearing a grim expression, returned to the table with two glasses of iced tea. "Just heard on the radio that a tornado struck some area in LaGrange. Doesn't sound like it's heading this way, though. But I'd keep an eye on the weather out there."

Delbert's eyes widened. "LaGrange? Ach, I hope my house is still standing."

Elma's heart pounded, and she squeezed her eyes shut. *Heavenly Father, please let everyone there be okay.*

CHAPTER 30

Grabill

D id ya hear the news about the tornado that hit LaGrange last night?" Dave asked when he picked Ben up to take him to a chiropractic appointment the following morning.

Eyes widening, Ben shook his head. "How bad was it? Did anyone get hurt?" He thought about the woman he'd delivered Mom's flowers to a few months back.

"There were several injuries, but I don't think any lives were lost." Dave's forehead creased. "Lots of destruction to some homes and barns in that area, though. I can only imagine what those poor families are going through today. They're gonna need help rebuilding."

Ben drew in a deep breath and blew it out quickly. "A group of Amish men from our area will likely go, and I plan to be with them."

Dave turned his head, looking at Ben through half-closed eyelids. "You sure your back's up to it? The pain you've been dealing with is the reason you're going to the chiropractor's, isn't it?"

Ben nodded. "I'm certain after Dr. Stevens works me over, I'll be good as new. Sure can't sit around here when there's work to be done and people are in need of our help. I'm gonna get there as quickly as possible."

⌒

LaGrange

Delbert rubbed a fist against his aching chest as he stared at the area where his house used to be. What had once been a cozy abode for him to live in was now nothing but a pile of rubble. Winds that had blown up to 180 miles per hour had wreaked havoc throughout several parts of his town.

"Thank the Lord you weren't at home when the tornado struck." Joseph draped his arm across Delbert's shoulder. "Most likely you would have been killed."

"It's strange to look at that heap of rubble and know it was once my house. I'd like to sift through it to see if there's anything worth salvaging." Delbert reached in his pocket for a hankie and wiped his nose. "The Lord giveth and He taketh away. It's all according to His plans, and maybe I'll have something better when it's all said and done. Jah, it could have been worse." He spread his arms open wide. "This can all be replaced. Guess my time here on earth isn't meant to be over just yet."

His good friend nodded. "The community will help you rebuild, as well as assist others in the area who lost their property. I have it on good authority that a crew from Topeka will be coming here later today to get started. And I'm sure other communities in the state, and perhaps beyond, will send workers, too."

Delbert's vision blurred as he held his arms close to his body. "I'll appreciate all the help I can get." He turned to face Joseph. "Danki for letting me stay at your house last night after I learned that my home was gone. Don't know what I'd do without a good friend like you."

Joseph's eyes welled with tears. "You'd do the same for me if the boot was on the other foot."

Delbert stared at the ground. Joe was right—there wasn't anything he wouldn't do to help his best friend.

⁓

Topeka

"With everything there is to do at the store, are you sure you want to go to LaGrange to help out?"

Thelma's question drove Elma's thoughts aside, and she set her paper and pen on the coffee table. "I am absolutely certain. Joseph and many other men from our area have gone there to help out, and they'll need to be fed. I'm sure there are other chores I can do there, too." She clasped her hands together. "Remember, Galatians 6:9 says:

'And let us not be weary in well doing: for in due season we shall reap, if we faint not.'"

"You're right. But what about the store? Who's going to take care of things there?" Thelma gestured to her little ones, sleeping peacefully in their playpen across the room. "I'd work in the store while you're gone, but I wouldn't get anything done if I took the bopplin along."

Elma smiled. "No, but they'd sure get a lot of attention from customers."

"True. So what are you going to do?"

Elma lifted her hands. "It's all taken care of. I asked Doris Miller if she'd help Lizzie while I'm gone, and she agreed. In fact, she's probably on her way now, since I'll be leaving soon."

"Will you be coming home each day?" Thelma asked.

"Most likely I'll stay. I can get more things done that way. Many people will open their homes for the workers, so I'm sure I'll find a place to stay at night."

"How many days will be you be there?"

Elma shrugged. "I don't know. As long as they need cooks, I'll stay—at least till someone comes along to replace me." Elma paused. "There is something you can do to help me, though. Will you watch my dog while I'm gone?"

"Of course. You can bring him over here when you're done packing."

"Danki. Between Doris and Lizzie, the cat will be taken care of, and they'll also feed and water my horse and the chickens. I made sure to warn the ladies about Hector, the feisty rooster. He can be a little schtinker. Hector almost got me the other day with his long spurs." Elma grimaced. "As usual, it gave me a scare, so I let Doris and Lizzie know to keep the broom handy."

Thelma smiled. "Good thinking. You wouldn't feel right if that naughty chicken hurt either of those nice women." She rolled her eyes. "Why don't you get rid of that despicable old chicken?"

"I'll admit, he's a handful, but the other chickens—especially the hens, get along fine with him."

"Well, it's nice of Lizzie and Doris to take care of the critters.

And please don't worry about Freckles. He can hang out here with Ginger for a few days."

"I bet he will enjoy having another dog to play with."

"It's a shame about Delbert's house." Thelma slumped in her chair. "I can't imagine how he must feel right now."

⌒

About an hour after Elma left, Freckles started to whine.

"It's okay, boy, she'll be back." Thelma felt sorry for the dog. He'd grown quite attached to Elma.

Freckles pawed at her leg, and she reached down to pat his head.

Ginger, who lay under the kitchen table, got up and drank some water from her dish. Thelma figured Freckles might follow suit, but he continued to sit at her feet and whine.

After a while, it got on her nerves. She went to the cupboard and got him a dog bone. Of course, Ginger's ears perked up and she had to have one, too. Their bodies poised, both dogs sat waiting for their tasty treat.

Thelma smiled while watching the dogs crunch on their bones. She enjoyed Joseph's dog, but since the twins were born, poor Ginger had taken a backseat. Maybe Ginger would gain more attention as Charles and Miriam grew.

After the dogs were through with their treats, Thelma heard the babies crying from the other room. It probably wouldn't be long before her sister's dog started whining again.

"How would you two like to go out in the yard and play?" Thelma moved toward the door.

Both dogs' ears perked up, and Ginger raced to the door. Freckles followed.

Thelma opened the door a crack and checked to see that the fence gate was closed before letting the dogs out. It was, so she opened it wider and was nearly knocked off her feet when Freckles and Ginger dashed outside.

Those silly critters. Shaking her head, she closed the door behind them and went to take care of the twins.

Sometime later, after the babies were fed and changed, Thelma heard scratching at the back door. When she opened it, she was surprised to see only Ginger on the porch.

She glanced around but saw no sign of Freckles.

"Here, Freckles! Come here, boy!" She clapped her hands.

No response.

"That's strange. I wonder if he found his way into the barn." Thelma stepped off the porch and was about to head in that direction when she noticed the fence gate hung open. "Oh, great! It must not have been securely latched."

She ran up to the fence and cupped her hands around her mouth. "Freckles! Where are you, boy?"

Not a sound and no sign of the dog.

Her heart pounded. *Oh, dear. That hund had better be back before Elma gets home.*

Elma had become attached to the dog and would be upset if she lost him. Even Delbert seemed to like Freckles. The last time they'd had him over for supper, he'd asked about the dog.

Thelma called for Freckles several more times but finally gave up and went inside. Hopefully by the time Elma returned, Freckles would be here waiting. If not, Thelma would have some explaining to do, and she didn't look forward to that.

Chapter 31

LaGrange

Elma took a break from the food table where she'd been helping ever since arriving a few hours ago. She pulled her shawl tightly around her shoulders, her heart heavy from all the devastation she saw. Despite the shawl's heaviness, Elma's body felt cold. But it wasn't the chilly March air causing her to tremble. It was the sight of so many somber-faced people who had lost their homes. Her heart ached for them.

It was surprising how the storm hit only certain houses but skipped others. For some, it was a miracle, but for the unfortunate ones like Delbert, not only had their homes been flattened, but bits and pieces of furniture and personal belongings were scattered everywhere.

One scene made Elma's eyes spill over with tears when she stopped to watch a little girl who'd found one of her dolls. Like a loving mother, the child rocked back and forth, comforting and whispering to her doll, holding it as gently as if it were a real baby.

Elma tore her gaze away as she took in more of the destruction. She noticed missing shingles and blown-out windows in several houses and barns. Tree branches lay scattered about, while some trees had been sheared off into stumps. Yet despite the rubble and mess, no lives had been lost, and only a few people were slightly injured. Temporary shelters had been set up in some of the buildings in town, and as Elma suspected, many people had opened their homes. Upon hearing of the disaster, Amish and English folks started working together to help those whose lives had been upended. Some brought in food, the way Elma did, while others offered supplies and began clearing debris and helping people put their homes back together.

"Thank You, God," she murmured, watching two Amish men working side by side with an English man who'd lost his barn.

She spotted Delbert talking to Joseph and hurried over to them. Elma could hardly believe the sight before her. Delbert's house was gone, as well as part of his woodworking shop. As horrible as it seemed, at least Delbert was alive and unhurt.

As Elma stepped up to Delbert, she was overcome with the need to give him a hug. Unsure of how he might take it, she placed her hand on his arm and gave it a tender squeeze. "I'm sorry for your loss." Her words seemed so insignificant, for she could not imagine the emotions going through him right now.

He dropped his gaze to the ground. "My home and material things can be replaced; I'm *dankbaar* to be alive."

"I am thankful, too." When Elma glanced to the right, her breath caught in her throat. Ben Wagler had come, and he was heading her way.

"Excuse me, Delbert, I see someone I know and should go say hello."

"Of course. Go right ahead."

She moved slowly toward Ben. "Wh–what are you doing here?" Elma could barely find her voice, and her gaze fixed on him. The sight of Ben coming toward her caused Elma to shiver even more. She noticed that he walked a bit slower than normal.

"Came to help out, like all the others." He motioned to a crew of men picking up debris. "I didn't expect to see you here, Elma."

She lifted her chin. "I came for the same reason you did. To help wherever I can." Elma pointed to the rubble that used to be Delbert's house. "My friend Delbert's home was one of the many places that were totally destroyed."

"Is he the man you were talking to?"

"Jah. Delbert and my brother-in-law have been friends a good many years."

"I see." He took a few steps toward her and winced.

"Are you okay?"

"My back's been acting up lately, but it's some better after seeing my chiropractor."

"Maybe you shouldn't have come." Elma bit the inside of her lip. "What if you injure your back even more?"

"There's a lot of work that needs to be done here, and I can help in many ways. Just have to watch myself." He stared at her, his eyes never moving. "It's good to see you, Elma. I've been wondering how you were doing." He reached out and touched her arm.

Goose bumps erupted all the way up to her neck. The mere sight of him filled Elma's heart with regrets. "I'm fine. How are you?"

"Other than my back, I'm doin' okay, I guess." He leaned on the table where the paper plates and cups had been set. "But I'd be even better if I was with you."

His bold statement caused her to jerk.

"Sorry if I offended you. It's just that—"

She shook her head briskly. "No, no, I wasn't offended. You took me by surprise."

His voice lowered as he leaned a bit closer. "Do you feel the same about me?"

Elma felt like a mouse caught between a cat's paws. Ben knew why they couldn't be together. Why was he bringing this up now?

She parted her lips, about to respond, when an exuberant German shorthair pointer showed up, out of nowhere, barking frantically and wagging his tail.

"Freckles!"

"Hunter!"

Ben and Elma spoke at the same time.

Elma looked at Ben and blinked.

"Freckles?" Ben tipped his head to the side. "Is this your dog, Elma? The one you told me about?"

Reaching down to pet the dog's head, Elma nodded. "But you just called him Hunter."

"Jah. This is my hund, I'm sure of it." Ben slapped his knee and called the dog. "Come here, Hunter. Come on, boy."

The dog darted over to Ben and pawed at his pant leg.

Elma clapped her hands. "Come here, Freckles! Come to me."

Obediently, the animal ambled over to her.

Elma's mouth opened wide. So did Ben's.

Ben pointed to the dog. "Where and when did you get him?"

"Delbert offered him to me several months ago." Elma looked toward Joseph and Delbert, down on their knees, sorting through the rubble. "The dog showed up at his house, and when he couldn't locate its owner, I volunteered to take him."

"So you named him Freckles?"

She bobbed her head. "With all his liver spots, it seemed like a fitting name."

Ben reached under his straw hat and scratched the side of his head. "I lost my hund when I was delivering flowers to a woman in LaGrange. The crazy critter jumped out of the truck, and after looking for him several hours with no luck, I finally gave up and went home."

"So the dog is yours, and his name is Hunter?"

"Jah." Ben motioned to the dog's collar. "I bought that for him last year."

Elma couldn't deny it was Ben's lost dog, but the idea of giving him up put an ache in her heart. "He's obviously your dog, but I can't figure out how he got here. I left him in Topeka with my sister this morning. Guess he must have gotten away somehow and run off—although I can't imagine what directed him here."

"I'm thinkin' he wanted to be with the two people he loves, so he sought us out." Ben offered a thumbs-up.

She giggled. "You really believe he could do that?"

"Sure do. I've heard of other dogs traveling farther than this to find their way back to their owner. And ya know what else, Elma?"

She shook her head.

"We can't make him choose between us, so as far as I can tell, there's only one answer to the problem."

"What would it be?"

"We're gonna have to get married so Hunter/Freckles can live with both of us."

Elma swallowed hard. "Ben, you know that's not possible. Your home is in Grabill, and mine's—"

He put his finger against her lips. "I can move to Topeka and start over."

She shook her head vigorously. "Oh no, Ben, I couldn't ask you to do that."

"You didn't ask. It was my suggestion."

"But your business is there, and so is your mamm. It wouldn't be fair to her if you moved."

"Mom can move with me. And if you need more assistance in the store, maybe she can help out. Who knows? After I retire from horseshoeing, you might put me to work in your store, too. With my back issues, I may not be shoeing horses much longer." Ben clasped Elma's arm. "Please say you'll at least think about it."

As far as Elma was concerned, there was nothing to think about. She would love it if Ben moved to Topeka and they got married. His mother, however, might not want to move—in which case, he should remain in Grabill to look after her needs.

She fiddled with her head-covering ties, weighing her choices. As much as Elma loved Ben, she had an obligation to Thelma, so moving to Grabill would be difficult, if not impossible.

Ben moved his hand from Elma's arm to take hold of her hand. "I believe God brought us together today for a reason, and our meeting and little mishap at the farmers' market in Shipshe last spring was no accident." He brought her hand to his lips and kissed it softly. Looking tenderly into Elma's eyes, Ben grew serious. "Maybe Hunter, or Freckles, did bring us together again today. I could use that as a reason, but truthfully speaking, I've been miserable ever since I received your letter. You have been on my mind since I first saw you, and there hasn't been a day since meeting you in Shipshe that I haven't thought of you. I've prayed that somehow we'd find each other again."

Elma's heart beat wildly when Ben took both of her hands. "Elma, I love you."

As if to reaffirm what he'd said, Hunter gave a loud *Woof! Woof!* before slurping both of their hands.

Elma was about to respond when Ben added, "As soon as I return home, I'm going to talk to my mamm. I feel confident she'll be willing to move. She knows how much I love you." Ben wet his lips and looked tenderly at Elma. "Will you marry me?"

Her mind racing as she thought of the possibility, all Elma could do was nod. *If Dorothy Wagler agrees to Ben's plan, I'll be forever grateful.*

Epilogue

One year later

Sitting beside her groom at their corner table, all Elma could think about was how fortunate she was to have met a man as wonderful as Ben. She smiled at him, as he looked so handsome in his wedding suit. He smiled in return and squeezed her fingers under the table. Elma's heart was filled with gratitude over his mother's willingness to move to Topeka. Everything had fallen into place, as though it was meant to be. An Amish couple with five children bought the Waglers' farm in Grabill, and Ben retired from horseshoeing. He would now be helping Elma run the store, and Dorothy would work part-time there, too, as well as Lizzie. This would allow Ben and Elma time off in order to go on trips or do other fun things together.

Elma glanced across the room to where her sister and brother-in-law sat eating their meal. Charlie sat on Joseph's lap, and Miriam was seated on Thelma's lap. Mom and Dad sat across from them, all smiles. Ben's mother was seated at another table, along with Ben's sister and her family. Everyone seemed to be having a good time, which only added to Elma's pleasure.

Her gaze went to Delbert, sitting at the same table with the widow Rachel Lambright and her seven-year-old son, Ryan. He'd begun courting her six months ago, and if things continued on the same path, Elma suspected before the year was out, they might be celebrating another wedding. She could tell Ryan was warming up to Delbert by the boy's big grin as the two interacted. Elma also noticed warm smiles being exchanged between Dell and Rachel. She was glad things were working out for her friend. After the tornado, with the help of those in the community and even outside the area, Delbert's house had been rebuilt in only a few weeks.

Despite the chilly March winds blowing outside Joseph's barn where the afternoon wedding meal was taking place, blue skies and puffy white clouds made the day perfect.

While Elma enjoyed the delicious meal with her new husband, Thelma got up from her seat and handed Miriam to her grandmother. Then she picked up a large wicker basket sitting on the floor and made her way to the wedding couple's table. Thelma placed it in front of them, and then, one by one, guests started filing up and putting pieces of fresh fruit inside.

Elma looked at Ben with her mouth gaping open as apples, oranges, bananas, and a few pears quickly had the basket full of colorful produce. After the last person came up to put fruit in the basket, Thelma topped it off with some deep purple grapes then gave Elma a big grin.

Elma smiled as her husband stood, cleared his throat, and started to thank everyone. His little speech no sooner got started when he gestured to the overflowing basket and accidentally bumped it with his hand. The basket toppled over, and all the vibrant fruit spilled out, bouncing and rolling off in different directions.

A hush went among the guests, but Ben was quick to say, "It's okay." He chuckled, bending down to pick up an apple then handing it to Elma. "This little mishap is a pleasant reminder of how we met at the farmers' market in Shipshewana two years ago." He smiled at Elma. "You were so kind to me that day when I made my little blunder. I could not be more fortunate to have found a woman who cares about others and goes around doing good. I feel truly blessed."

"And I've never grown weary of following the Lord's example, for in due season, I truly have reaped a blessed reward." Tears welled in her eyes as she looked at her groom. "And I, too, feel doubly blessed."

ELMA'S HEALTHY BLUEBERRY CRISP

Ingredients:

5 cups fresh or frozen
  blueberries
1¼ cups coconut sugar,
  divided
2 tablespoons instant tapioca

½ cup water
1 teaspoon lemon juice
½ cup melted butter
1 cup gluten-free flour
1 cup gluten-free quick oats

Combine berries, ¾ cup coconut sugar, tapioca, water, and lemon juice. Pour into greased 9x13 baking dish. In bowl, mix butter, ½ cup coconut sugar, flour, and oats. Sprinkle over blueberry mixture. Bake at 350 degrees for 40 minutes. Serve plain or with vanilla ice cream or whipped topping.

Thelma's Tasty Potato Salad

Ingredients:
12 cups potatoes, boiled
12 eggs, boiled
2 cups celery, chopped
1½ cups onion, chopped
3 cups mayonnaise

3 tablespoons vinegar
3 tablespoons mustard
4 teaspoons salt
1½ cups sugar
½ cup milk

Shred cooked potatoes and eggs into bowl. Add celery and onion. In separate bowl, mix mayonnaise, vinegar, mustard, salt, sugar, and milk. Pour over potato mixture and combine gently. Best when made up the day before or several hours before serving.

New York Times bestselling and award-winning author **Wanda E. Brunstetter** is one of the founders of the Amish fiction genre. Wanda's ancestors were part of the Anabaptist faith, and her novels are based on personal research intended to accurately portray the Amish way of life. Her books are well read and trusted by many Amish, who credit her for giving readers a deeper understanding of the people and their customs. When Wanda visits her Amish friends, she finds herself drawn to their peaceful lifestyle, sincerity, and close family ties. Wanda enjoys photography, ventriloquism, gardening, bird-watching, beachcombing, and spending time with her family. She and her husband, Richard, have been blessed with two grown children, six grandchildren, and two great-grandchildren. To learn more about Wanda, visit her website at www.wandabrunstetter.com.

Jean Brunstetter became fascinated with the Amish when she first went to Pennsylvania to visit her father-in-law's family. Since that time, Jean has become friends with several Amish families and enjoys writing about their way of life. She also likes to put some of the simple practices followed by the Amish into her daily routine. Jean lives in Washington State with her husband, Richard Jr., and their three children, but she takes every opportunity to visit Amish communities in several states. In addition to writing, Jean enjoys boating, gardening, and spending time on the beach.

Let's Keep In Touch!

Want to know what Wanda's up to and be the first to hear about new releases, specials, the latest news, and more? Like Wanda on Facebook!

 Visit facebook.com/WandaBrunstetterFans